T0164503

the buddha's story

the buddha's story

chris matheson

PITCHSTONE PUBLISHING
DURHAM, NORTH CAROLINA

Pitchstone Publishing
Durham, North Carolina
www.pitchstonebooks.com
Copyright © 2020 by Chris Matheson

Library of Congress Cataloging-in-Publication Data

Names: Matheson, Chris, author.
Title: The Buddha's story / Chris Matheson.
Description: Durham, North Carolina : Pitchstone Publishing, [2020] |
    Summary: "A humorous take on the life of Siddhartha Gautama, imagined
    as an autobiography written by him, spanning from his birth to his eventual
    so-called extinction"— Provided by publisher.
Identifiers: LCCN 2019054124 (print) | LCCN 2019054125 (ebook) |
    ISBN 9781634312004 (hardcover) | ISBN 9781634312011 (ebook)
Subjects: LCSH: Gautama Buddha—Fiction. | Monks—India—Fiction.
Classification: LCC PS3613.A8262 B83 2020 (print) | LCC PS3613.A8262
    (ebook) | DDC 813/.6—dc23
LC record available at https://lccn.loc.gov/2019054124
LC ebook record available at https://lccn.loc.gov/2019054125

"Your Holiness, tell me, what role does
Jesus Christ play in your Muslim religion?"

—*Larry King, in a rather awkward interview
with the 14th Dalai Lama, a living Buddha of compassion*

"I'm sorry, but could you please repeat the question?"

—*The 14th Dalai Lama*

* The much-hyped interview was broadcast live on December 31,
1999 as part of CNN's Millennium 2000 primetime coverage. Al-
though the exchange was watched by millions, neither the full video
nor the official transcript has ever been posted online—almost as if
the entire interview is meant to be completely forgotten. Thus, as with
the life of Siddhartha himself, the exact truth about the interview that
night may be lost to history. Yet, the story of it lives on as legend.

abbreviations

KSJAT—King Shibi Jataka

AVDS—Avadanasataka

NK—Nidanakatha

SV—Sangityavamsa

ASV—Asvaghosha

KDS—Kinh Duoc Su

MJ—Majjhima Nikaya

GV—Gandavyuha

ACC—Acchariya-abhutta Sutra

MHP—Mahapadana Sutra

ATT—Atthakavagga

LV—Lalitavistara Sutra

IDD—Iddhipada-vibanga Sutra

DP—Dhammapada

RH—Rhinoceros Horn Sutra

ITI—Itivattaka

AP—Ariyapariyesana Sutra

SK—Sukhavativyuha Sutra

SAL—Saleyyana Sutra

MH—Mahasaccaka Sutra

SY—Samyutta Nikaya

HJAT—Hare Jataka

ANG—Anguttara Nikaya

MV—Mahavagga

DCP—Dhammacakkappavattana Sutra

DG—Digha Nikaya

SP—Satipatthana Sutra

PP—Padopama Sutra

TV—Theravada Vinaya

VK—Vimalikirti Sutra

TGG—Tathagatagharba Sutra

OJO—Ojoyoshu

SZJ—Sishier Zhang Jing

ILL—Illumination of the Five Realms

LSV—Larger Sukhavativyuha

PV—Petavatthu

SH—Shurangama Sutra

AGG—Agganna Sutra

SDS—Saddhamasmrtyupasthana Sutra

DFMHG—Deliverance from Flaming
      Mouth Hungry Ghost Sutra

SOA—Sermon on Abuse

MHD—Mahadukkhakhanda Sutra

GPJAT—Golden Peacock Jataka

MGD—Magandiya Sutra

GTJAT—Goblin Town Jataka

PP—Parajika Pei

IOU—Inquiry of Ugra

CV—Cullavagga

MSV—Mulasarvastivada Sutra

BL—Bimba's Lament

FCJAT—Fairy Canda Jataka

NKV—Nandakovada Sutra

RUJAT—Rupyavati Jataka

RAH—Rahulovada Sutra

VSJA—Vessantara Jataka

MUS—Parable of the Mustard Seed

THR—Therigatha

CMJAT—Crocodile and Monkey Jataka

MCJAT—Marsh Crow Jataka

UD—Udana

JBJAT—Jackal Beware Jataka

SYEJAT—Sixty Year Old Elephant Jataka

JTMKJAT—Jolly the Monkey King Jataka

OEJAT—Obedient Elephant Jataka

NKR—Nihon Ryoi Ki

SDI—Sanghadisesa

CCJAT—Compassionate Captain Jataka

MPB—Mahaparinibbana Sutra

LOT—Lotus Sutra

CSG—Chan School Gonyan

PMKS—Phra Malai Klon Suat

NBS—Nembutsu Shu

BA—Buddha Amitayus

SSV—Smaller Sukhavativyuha

WTJAT—Wishing Tree Jataka

LJJAT—Lion and Jackal Jataka

BYJAT—Brahmin Youth Jataka

part i: beginning

1

I am the Buddha and this is my story.

To begin with, I want to give you an idea of the greatness of my essential nature. In one of my many previous lifetimes, I was a king named Shibi. As King Shibi, I was so brimming over with compassion that merely in order to feed a bird (a pigeon to be precise) I cut off all of my own flesh, thereby becoming a skeleton. I remember slicing all my flesh away, then standing proudly and proclaiming, "I sacrifice my body not for treasure but for enlightenment, in order that I may save all living beings!" At that point, I recited a kind of a poem, which went something like this:

> *Dragons and demons and gods and ghosts*
> *I am a hero and that is no boast*
> *Singers and dancers and ogres and fools*
> *You should be like me and follow my rules.*

I did not mean, quite obviously, that gods, ghosts, etc. should all be talking skeletons like me. Rather, what I meant was that they should all wish to be motivated by pure, selfless compassion like I was. In heaven, the gods were so impressed by my sacrifice that they cheered enthusiastically. "Bravo!" they all cried. "*BRAVO FOR THE TALKING SKELETON!*" After that, it rained flowers on my bones, which was nice. (KSJAT.)

Here is another example of how noble I was in a previous lifetime: As King Padmaka, I was a good and loving ruler who cared tenderly for his dear subjects. When a deadly plague struck my kingdom and it turned out that the only thing that could possibly save my people was the flesh of an extremely rare fish known as the Rohita, I instantly decided to kill myself and be reborn as that fish in order that I might allow myself to be eaten. I remember climbing to the top of my palace, throwing down some incense and flowers, praying, "Make me the Rohita fish!" and jumping. I died the moment I hit the ground and was instantly reborn as the Rohita fish, as I obviously knew I would be. (I wouldn't have jumped off the roof of my palace otherwise.)

Now that I was the Rohita fish, my people came at me with spears and hooks and started slicing me to pieces while I was still alive. As they chopped me up, I wept tears of love for them and cried out, "Eat of my flesh, citizens, eat and be healed!" They proceeded to feast on my body for the next twelve years. (The Rohita is an enormous fish.) At the end of those twelve years I cried out to my people once more: "I, YOUR KING PADMAKA, HAVE *SAVED* YOU!" (How I could still speak after they'd been eating me for twelve consecutive years, I am still not quite sure, but I definitely could.) (AVDS)

I will now tell you the story of my final and greatest lifetime, the one in which I finally became the Buddha. It all began in Tusita Heaven, the lovely place I had lived for several hundred years. One day some gods came to me and begged me to reenter human life. I remember their exact words to me: "Sir," they said (because the gods always treated me as their superior, which I was), "now that you have achieved perfection you must save mankind. Now, sir, is the time for your Buddhahood." (NK; SV)

Before I agreed to go to earth, I needed to survey the situation. "First of all," I remember thinking, "I must be born into a superior and wealthy family. My mother must not be a slutty drunk. That woman down there, Queen Maya, looks more than acceptable." At that point, I turned to the gods. "I guess this is goodbye, old friends," I said, then walked into Tusita City Park and flew down to earth. (NK)

I was conceived in the following way: In a dream, my mother was anointed with perfume and covered with flowers. I then took the form of a multi-tusked, heavily perfumed white elephant and entered her womb. (NK; ASV. 1:20) Q: Does this mean that I *was* a white elephant? A: No, it certainly does not mean that. Nor does it mean that my *father* was a white elephant and that I was therefore half white elephant. Q: What *does* it mean then? A: That I briefly took the *shape* of a white elephant as I entered my mother's womb, achieving what you might call "Poetic Effect."

White Elephant-Me quickly informed my mother that she was pregnant. "You have conceived a pure and powerful being," I told her from within her womb. (The moment I was conceived, by the way, the following things occurred: Hunchbacks stood upright, the fires in hell briefly went out and basically everyone in the world was in an excellent mood. (NK) Similarly, when I was born ten months later, the mute sang and the lame danced. How long they continued to do so after my birth, I cannot say. They might've sang and danced only for a few moments and then reverted to their lameness and dumbness.) (KDS)

When I took up residence in my mother's womb, four gods joined me in order to make sure that no one should harm me. (MJ 123) Some people later claimed that *billions* of other Buddhas lived in my mother's womb with me, that my mother was somehow the mother of all Buddhas, past, present and future. This is absolutely untrue. My mother's womb was not, as some people later said, "as vast as the heavens" nor was it "as huge as outer space." People didn't *walk around* in my mother's womb, taking "steps as big as star systems." There were no "bejewelled *palaces*" in Mother's womb and I definitely wasn't sitting in one of them being worshipped by 80,000 "Snake Kings," led by one particular reptile named "Sagara!" (GV 44) *None* of that is true.

As I was born, the four gods caught me in a little net. I exited my mother's side because, needless to say, I was *not* going to be corrupted by the loathsome impurities of her birth canal. (ASV 1:25–32) I emerged pure, clean and shiny, like a precious little gem, which is exactly what I was. (ACC 3:118–24) I actually *walked* out of mother's side like a little man striding down a staircase, arms swinging free and easy, until I fell into the gods' net. I didn't need to be bathed after my birth because, as I just mentioned, I was born completely free of all "vaginal impurities." Nevertheless, as an extra precaution apparently, two jets of water sprayed down on me from the heavens, one of them cool, the other warm. After that (for the first, but definitely not the last time) flowers were dumped on me. (NK; ASV 1:29)

As soon as my shower was over, I jumped out of the gods' net, stood up and looked around. "No one is superior to you," the gods cried to me. "How *could* they be?" I gazed around in every direction and, seeing no one equal to me, took several large steps forward. (Brahma, the main god present, hurried alongside me holding a little white parasol over my head to shield me from the sun, which was considerate of him.) I suddenly stopped, pointed one hand at the ground and the other at the sky and proclaimed at the top of my little lungs, *"I AM THE KING OF THE WORLD!"* (NK; ACC 3:118–24)

After that, I looked directly at my mother and announced, "This will be my final birth. After this lifetime I will achieve *extinction*." (ASV 1:34) At that point, my mother passed out. A few days later, she died. This was a sad turn of events, of course, but also, to be honest, necessary. My mother's womb, you see, was like a little shrine to me. After I was born, no other being could inhabit it without contaminating it. Consequently, Mother had to die. Luckily for me, Mother's sister, my Aunt Prajapati, stepped in and raised me, acting as a surrogate mother. I was not deprived in any way. (NK; MHP)

I was given the name "Siddhartha," which means "Every Wish Fulfilled," because that, in fact, was to be my destiny. I was born to dispel ignorance, help mankind move beyond pain and suffering and end the misery of all living things in the universe. I was born, that is, to be the most profound conqueror the world has ever known, the conqueror of *anguish*.

Thus my life began.

2

Not long after my mother died, my father, King Suddhodana, invited a group of seers to his palace to predict my future. It was obvious to everyone that I was a *special* child; I had, after all, emerged from my mother's side, dashed around and announced that I was the King of the World. My "specialness" was not in question. The only question was: What *kind* of king would I be, worldly or spiritual?

The seers informed my father that if I ever left his palace and observed what the outside world was like, I would become a spiritual ruler. If, on the other hand, I remained within the palace's cloistered walls, I would become a worldly ruler. Father decided to keep me in the palace, so there I grew up in pampered luxury, surrounded by every kind of wealth and beauty imaginable, never exposed to ugliness of any kind. (NK) Father indulged my every whim. I had a charming little golden carriage which was pulled by four deer, for instance. (ASV 2:22–29) My bedroom was decorated like a heavenly chariot.

With regard to my physical perfection, well, where to even begin? My voice had sixty-four different pitches, all of them extremely pleasing to the ear; I mainly sounded like a bird (a sparrow), which is a splendid thing for a human boy to sound like. I could touch my ear-holes with my tongue; I could also lick my own forehead; I had magnificently webbed fingers and toes; I had wheels on my feet; my head was shaped like a turban. (That last one might not sound good, but it looked fantastic, I assure you.) I also had perfect judgment. An example: When seasoning foods, I knew exactly, and I mean *exactly,* the right amount of seasoning to add for optimal eating pleasure. (MJ 91; ASV 1:65; MHP)

To be clear, I have no "ego" about any of these things. I state them merely as facts. The truth is that I long ago transcended ego (ATT 1:11–15); I do not even have an ego—I am interested only in love and compassion. (MJ 90) But it is undeniably the case that I was a dazzling and wondrous boy. Everything came easily to me. I could master any subject without any instruction. I spoke sixty-four different languages, each with its own alphabet. I was extremely gifted at mathematics. I once informed my father that I could count all the atoms in the world. Father, justifiably amazed, said, "That is a lot of atoms, son." "Yes, it certainly is, Father," I agreed. "Will that not take you a very long time, Siddhartha?" "No, Father, in fact, I can do it in the time it takes you to draw a single breath!" That left Father speechless. (LV 10–12)

I was also a brilliant archer. One time I entered an archery tournament (which is amusing in a way because, honestly, why would *anyone* think they could beat me?) and I was just about to shoot when I stopped and turned to the crowd. "With this bow of meditative concentration," I announced to them, "I will fire the arrow of wisdom and kill the tiger of ignorance in all living beings!" I still remember how impressed people were by my eloquence. I then fired my arrow, which flew straight through an iron wall before disappearing deep in the earth. (LV 10–12) "The young prince is a wonderment," the people all proclaimed. Which again, ego aside, I was.

As I have mentioned, Father did not want me to know that suffering existed. For that reason, sickness, old age and death were strictly forbidden from my presence. As soon as a servant hit the age of forty or so they were quickly removed from the palace, as was anyone who got ill. I remember observing a man sneeze one day and thinking to myself, "What was *that* about?" and then noticing that the man was gone the next day. Even ugly people were banned from my sight. Only healthy and beautiful young people were allowed to be near me. And it wasn't just people either. If a goat got sick, it was quickly slaughtered. Even plants were treated this way; if they wilted even slightly, they were instantly uprooted. "Are you getting *older?*" I remember once asking my father. "Not at all," he responded. "Are you wearing *make-up?*" I continued. "Of course not," he huffed, though in hindsight he obviously was.

Sometimes I look back and wonder: Did I *actually* not grasp that people aged and got sick? Did I not notice myself aging? Did I myself never get sick? Could I have actually reached nearly thirty years of age without realizing that *death* existed? The truth is, there *was* some small inner part of me that sensed there was more to life than eternal health, youth and happiness. Glimpses of truth, that is, did occasionally break through.

The first one occurred when I was eight years old. There was a planting ceremony of some sort taking place. It was a very hot day, the sun was beating down. I sat in the shade of an apple tree observing the ceremony and as I sat there, I slowly went into a kind of trance. In hindsight, I understand that this was the first time I ever entered into the state of Oneness. The gods, perhaps impatient for me to begin saving the world, apparently wanting me to *remain* in this state of Oneness as long as possible, literally stopped the sun from moving for several hours, thus allowing me to remain comfortably in the shade. (NK)

Another important childhood epiphany: I was ten years old this time, once again sitting under an apple tree. (I was drawn to sitting under trees from the start.) A bird swooped down and pecked the ground near me, then flew away with a worm in its beak and I remember thinking to myself at that moment: "The worm will die." This led to the following question: "Does that mean *everything* will die?" Instantly I knew the answer: Of course everything would die. I felt a profound wave of sadness at this realization. "Things *die*," I whispered to myself. "*And before they die, they suffer.*"

A few years after that, I married the beautiful Princess Yasodhara. Father assumed that Yasodhara and I would quickly have children but thirteen years flew by and we remained childless. Why, you wonder? Because I was not ready to be a father, that's why. For that reason I did not lie with Yasodhara, not even one time. Trying to pique my interest in women, Father surrounded me with scantily clad dancing girls—a lot of them—40,000, to be exact. (NK) But the dancing girls' presence didn't work on me; I was too strong, I resisted. I had zero intention of creating a screaming little red-faced baby, because why on earth would I want *that*? (Also, to be honest, Yasodhara bled every month, which I found sickening.)

One night when I was in my late twenties, however, Yasodhara got the better of me. She poured wine for me, glass after glass, until I could barely see straight. She then pressed her body against me and whispered provocative things in my ear and before I knew it the dismal deed had taken place. I had kept my wife at bay for twelve years, but that one night I was weak and wouldn't you know it, the worst possible thing happened: Yasodhara got pregnant. (NK)

3

At that point I remember beginning to feel restless, trapped in Father's palace. "I need to grow up, Father," I remember saying to him one day. "When I was born I announced that I was the King of the World and now here I am, nearly thirty years old and spending my days lying in my chariot-themed bed, wearing my favorite golden helmet!"

"But you love your golden helmet, Siddhartha."

"I *do* love it, Stepmother, but that is not the point. The point is that there *must* be something more to life than *this.*"

"Would you like to redesign your bedroom, son?" Father asked me. "Make it look more like a dragon's lair, as you have sometimes mentioned?"

"No, Father, that is not at ALL what I want," I cried out, stomping away in frustration.

"Where are you going, Siddhartha?" Father called after me.

"I am going for a chariot ride!"

An hour later, accompanied by my driver, Chandaka, I was riding around the palace grounds in my best golden chariot. All my horses, including my (by *far*) favorite steed, Kamthaka, were wearing gold. (ASV 3:8) I was wearing my usual outfit: silks and jewels. My hair was long, flowing and frankly magnificent, topped with my finest helmet, which was decorated with golden lightning bolts.

As Chandaka drove us around the palace grounds, the citizens lined up and threw flowers at me. "They love me for my marvelous personality and conspicuous beauty, Chandaka," I announced. (ASV 3:11) "Yes, my lord."

As we neared our typical "turnaround" spot, an impulse suddenly came over me. "*Exit the palace gates*," I commanded Chandaka.

"But my lord, we are not supposed to do that."

"Do as I say, Chandaka."

"But your father—"

"Exit the palace gates NOW, Chandaka."

"As you wish, my lord."

Five minutes later, we were driving through the city outside the gates. It looked different than anyplace I'd ever been before, shabbier, more broken down and drab. I was studying a decaying building when I suddenly gasped. On the side of the road was a hunched-over old man, white-haired and extremely wrinkly. "What on earth *is* that creature?" I whispered to Chandaka. (ASV 3:28)

"It is an old man, my lord."

"What do you mean, 'old man'?" I demanded as I stared at the withered creature limping along with the help of a wooden staff.

"Things age, my lord," Chandaka said. "Did you *actually* not know that?"

I turned and looked Chandaka in the eye. "Will *I* age too?"

Chandaka averted his eyes. "*Chandaka,*" I demanded. "*Tell me, Chandaka.*"

"Everything ages, my lord," he murmured.

Oh, how my great soul shuddered when I heard that! (ASV 3:34) I looked around at the people on the street, many of whom were laughing and talking. "Why are they not *horrified,* Chandaka? How can they *live* with this dreadful knowledge?"

"Perhaps they are accustomed to the idea of getting older, my lord."

"Well, I am not accustomed to it, Chandaka. I am not in the LEAST accustomed to it! Honestly, how am I supposed to take pleasure in life again, knowing that I will get *old*?"

"Perhaps we should head back to the palace now, my lord."

"No, Chandaka, no. I need to know the truth about life. I *will* know the truth about life."

Five minutes later, we came upon a second horrid sight. A pale man with a swollen belly and open sores was shaking and muttering "mother" over and over again as he staggered along the road. (ASV 3:41) (This man didn't actually "exist," by the way. Neither had the "old man"; they were both just creations of the gods, meant to get my attention. Which they definitely did!)

"What is wrong with that man?" I whispered to Chandaka in amazement.

"He is sick, my lord."

"Sick?? What on earth do you mean 'sick'?"

"His body is ailing, my lord. He is in pain."

"Are you telling me that humans experience *pain*, Chandaka?"

"Have you yourself never experienced pain, my lord?"

"Oh, *I* have, obviously, but other people feel it too?" Before Chandaka could answer, I cried out, "Stop the chariot immediately—I wish to talk to this man!" Chandaka did so and I jumped out of my seat and hurried to the sick man. I stared at him for a moment, then said, "Does it hurt to be sick?"

"Yes, my lord, it hurts very much."

"How do you go on?"

"It is sometimes difficult, my lord."

"I can imagine. How could you enjoy life with such disgusting open sores on your body? Honestly I can't stand even having to look at the disgusting sores on your body."

"My lord," Chandaka said quietly, coming up behind me, "we really must return to the palace. Your father will not be pleased about this."

"Never *mind* my father, Chandaka, I am not a child, I am a full-grown *man* and I told you I need to understand the world.

We *will* continue."

As we got back into the carriage, I looked at the people passing by on the street. "Why do they look so *happy*, Chandaka? Are they *deluded?* YOU'RE ALL GOING TO GET SICK!!" I yelled at the people.

A few minutes later we hit the worst sight of all. Turning a corner, I saw people huddled in a doorway, crying.

"This one we should pass by, my lord," Chandaka muttered.

"Why?"

"This one is . . . exceedingly difficult."

"What do you *mean*, Chandaka?"

"Please let us keep going, my lord."

"What are all those people doing?"

"They are crying, my lord."

"You there—why do you cry? Stop, Chandaka!"

"We have lost our mother, sir."

"Yes, well, I lost my mother too," I replied, exiting the chariot again. "She died to preserve the sanctity of her womb after I was born, but I never *cried* about it."

I pushed through the weeping people, through a small hallway and into a main room, where I suddenly stopped. There, on a table before me, garlanded with flowers, laid a stiff, grey corpse. (The gods had created this corpse too obviously; she was kind of a "dummy" who had never actually "lived.") As I stared down at the dead body, I felt like I couldn't breathe, like time itself had stopped and I had been standing in that spot for an eternity. In truth, it was probably five seconds before Chandaka was beside me, whispering, "We must go now, my lord."

"This woman is *dead*, isn't she, Chandaka?"

"Yes, my lord."

"Because things *die*, don't they?"

"Yes, my lord."

"It's not only worms, is it?"

"No, my lord, it is all things."

"Which means—*I* will die, doesn't it, Chandaka?"

"Please, my lord . . ."

"I will die, *won't I, Chandaka? I WILL DIE, WON'T I??
TELL ME!*"

Chandaka finally nodded. "Death is the fate of all living
things, my lord."

"*Of course it is,*" my mind fairly shouted. *"How could it be
otherwise? Worms die, plants die, everything dies, **including me.**"* As
Chandaka started to lead me out of the room, hot tears streamed
down my noble face. "I'm going to DIE, Chandaka," I found
myself moaning as he led me back to the chariot. "*I,* Prince
Siddhartha, the King of the World, am going to DIIIIEEE!"
Feeling both helpless and enraged, I sank down into my seat and
glared balefully at the people passing by. "Why do you look so
happy, you fools?? I AM GOING TO DIE, *I AM GOING TO
DIIIEEEEE!*" (ASV 3:58–61)

It all came together then. Life was *pain.* That was all life
was, **pain.** I rode in silence, feeling the weight of this profound
insight. Finally Chandaka looked over at me. "Are you alright,
my lord?"

"No, Chandaka, I am *not* alright. I am frankly overwhelmed
by the hideous sights I have been subjected to! So much *pain,*
Chandaka."

"Yes."

"So much suffering."

"Indeed, my lord."

"How am I supposed to enjoy feasting on savory grilled
meats or drinking fine chilled wines or sniffing sweet perfumes
after seeing all of these vile things, Chandaka?"

"I do not know, my lord."

"Get me back to the palace," I moaned in despair.

But the gods had one final sight they needed me to see. As
we reapproached the palace gates, there, sitting by the side of the
road, close enough for me to touch, sat a small, thin man with
a shaved head. He was wearing a yellow robe and holding an
empty wooden bowl. As we slowly drove past him, I turned to

Chandaka. "What is he?"

"He is an 'ascetic,' my lord."

"'Ascetic'? What does it mean?"

"It means that he has renounced all worldly goods, my lord."

"Why?"

"In search of inner peace, my lord."

Those two words, "inner peace," had a profound effect on me. I suddenly grabbed the reins from Chandaka and stopped the chariot right next to the ascetic. (NK) I stared at the skinny little man, who sat calmly, a gentle smile on his weathered face. "Old man," I said to him. He nodded back at me. "You look quite wise."

"I am merely a seeker, young prince," the ascetic replied. Then he lowered his voice to something just above a whisper: "*As you too soon will be.*"

"How do you know *that*?"

"It is your *destiny*, young prince."

4

By the time I got back to the palace I was overwhelmed with emotion. Seeing me rush past, Father instantly understood what had happened. "You went into the city, didn't you, Siddhartha?"

I stopped, stared coldly at him. "Did you actually think I *wouldn't,* Father?"

"I assumed you would when you were sixteen or seventeen, twenty at the very latest. When you didn't do it then, no, I figured you wouldn't."

"Well, I *did,* Father. And by the way, why on earth did you think a king would be better off not knowing about suffering?"

"I didn't think you could handle it, son."

"Well guess what, I CAN handle it—you were wrong about that! Not only can I 'handle it,' I can *save* people from it!"

"How will you do that?"

"I don't know yet, but I will!"

"Siddhartha, stop."

"Leave me ALONE, Father!" I cried as I lurched past him and rushed upstairs to my room where I threw myself onto my chariot-themed bed and wept for hours.

Wanting to console me, Father sent dancing girls to my chambers. "Use your coquettishness to enrapture him," he instructed them. (ASV 4:9–12) Some of the girls crept into my bed and began pressing their breasts against me. One of them whispered, "Perform your rites of adoration *here,* young prince," hotly in my ear. When I leapt out of bed, another chesty woman stood in front of me, shook her earrings back and forth, then laughed and cried out in a merry voice, "Catch me if you can!" as she ran off. (ASV 4:32–39) I did not chase her, needless to say. I ducked into my closet and hid there, trembling with rage, one thought circling endlessly in my mind: "I WILL DIE. I WILL *DIE.* I WILL DIE."

Suddenly furious, I yanked back the closet curtain and glowered at the busty harlots and screamed at them.

"You laugh and sport and carry on," I cried, "but before long all of you will get *old* and *sick* and then you will DIE, YES, *ALL OF YOU* WILL DIE!!" One of the women, the one who'd been shaking her earrings at me, frowned. "You're being extremely rude, young prince," she said. Another dancing girl nodded.

"Obviously we know we're going to get old and sick and then die, young prince, who *doesn't* know that?" "Until today, ME!" I bellowed at them. "NOW GET OUT OF MY ROOM, GET OUT RIGHT NOW!!" After they left I cried myself to sleep.

The next morning I stood before Father and announced, "I wish to leave the palace."

"What do you mean?"

"I wish to become an ascetic in order that I may achieve enlightenment and fulfill my true destiny of saving the world."

"Go forth as an ascetic when you are *older,* Siddhartha, you are too young now."

"I am nearly thirty years old, Father."

"As I said, too young."

I looked at my father, nodded. "If you can promise me four things, Father, I will stay here at the palace."

"Anything, my son, anything at all—tell me."

"Can you promise to stop sickness, old age, pain and death, Father? If so, I will stay." (ASV 5:35)

"I cannot possibly stop those things, my son. You know that."

"*Exactly*, and that is why I must leave and find the answers for myself. Goodbye, Father."

As I started to turn away: "You will not survive out there, Siddhartha, you are a *boy*."

"I am twenty-nine years old, Father!"

"You are soft, my son. You are not built to endure hardship!"

"I am far tougher than you realize, Father."

"I'm sorry, Siddhartha, but I cannot allow you to leave."

"Father—"

He nodded to his guards. "Take him back to his chambers."

I shook my head in disbelief as they grabbed my arms. "It is not right to stop someone who wishes to escape from a house on *fire*, Father." (ASV 5:37)

"But this house is not on fire, Siddhartha."

"It *is* on fire, Father—ALL houses are on fire, LIFE ITSELF is on fire—and I am telling you that I *must* find a way to extinguish that fire!"

"This moment will pass, my son, you will see. Before long you will thank me for this."

An hour later, I sat on my bed glaring at my two guards and trying to figure out what to do next. Suddenly I realized something incredible: I could turn invisible! (IDD) I quickly did so and slipped out the door. I stopped, passing the large room where my dancing girls stayed. Standing in the doorway, I gazed at their sleeping forms. What I saw was, in a word, disgusting. Some of the women had saliva running out of the corners of their mouths; others were weirdly *covered* with saliva, as if they had been licking themselves. A few women laid there with wide, gaping mouths, while others were snoring or gnashing their teeth. One woman laid there half-naked, her skirt hitched up, her legs spread. "That is *monstrous*," I remember thinking to myself as I looked at her. "All you so-called beauties are not so beautiful now, are you?" I muttered to myself. "You are nauseating, in fact. And before long, you will be even more nauseating because before long you will be *dead*, you will be stinking, rotting corpses!" (NK; ASV 5:59–63)

"Everything is impermanent," I remember whispering to myself at that moment. "There is only one permanent thing in life and that is *pain*." The point of existence, I suddenly grasped, was escaping that pain. *But how to do it?*

That is what I now had to figure out.

5

Oh yes, there was one other thing that happened that week: My son Rahula was born. I named him "Rahula" because it means "shackle" and from the moment he was born, I knew that's what Rahula was going to be to me, a shackle. (DP 345–46) (Not that it matters, but Rahula's birth was grotesque. When I was born, there had been no blood at all, I was born pristine, like a perfect little gem. Rahula's birth, I regret to say, was *nothing* like that, it was bloody, messy and hideous.)

Yasodhara's door was open as I crept past the chamber where she dozed with our newborn baby asleep on her chest. The lamps in her room were burning low. There was the smell of scented oil and flowers were strewn across her bed. I slipped into the room, stared down at Rahula and shook my head sadly. This child's life, like all lives, would be filled with nothing but pain and *I* was responsible for it. There was only one thing for me to do and I knew it: "I am leaving," I whispered to the baby. "You are a shackle that binds me but now I am cutting you off." (SV)

Yasodhara woke up and looked at me. "Siddhartha?" she whispered. "Why do you look so strange, husband?"

"I am going forth into the world, Yasodhara."

She went up one elbow, rubbed her eyes. "'Going forth,' what does that mean?"

"I am going to live in the forest as an ascetic."

"But . . . I don't understand. When are you doing this?"

"Now. Tonight."

"And . . . when are you returning?"

"Never."

Her eyes widened. "But Siddhartha . . . what about Rahula, what about our son?"

"It is unfortunate that Rahula exists, Yasodhara. It would be far better if he didn't."

"Siddhartha, don't *say* that."

"But I will not be shackled by him or anyone else, Yasodhara. I henceforth declare myself free of all attachments, for it is only when one's attachments are extinguished that one's delusions can be extinguished." (RH)

"Siddhartha, *I love you.*"

"And I love all living things."

"Does that not include *me?*"

"It does, yes, but no more than that insect on the wall over there."

"How can you be so cruel, husband?"

"I have a destiny to meet, Yasodhara. It would be cruel of me not to do so." I started to rise. "I am leaving now."

Yasodhara grabbed my arm, desperate. "*Husband, please.* Stay with us. Think of your son, husband—your SON." (ASV 8:68)

"Rahula will die, Yasodhara, as will you, as will I. *All* of us will die."

"But while we are here, can we not *live,* husband*?*"

"What you are describing would be akin to pouring perfume onto a corpse."

"*Oh god.*"

"Farewell, Yasodhara."

With that, I turned and walked out of her chamber. It was the proudest moment of my life up to that point.

"Chandaka," I whispered, five minutes later.

" . . . My lord?" Chandaka responded thickly, half-turning to me in his bed.

"Wake up, we are leaving immediately. Get Kamthaka ready."

"But my lord—"

"*I said immediately, Chandaka*. It is time for me to attain **immortality**." (ASV 5:68)

"Yes, my lord."

Kamthaka looked marvelous that night, decked out as he was all in gold, with little tinkly bronze bells all over him. Kamthaka was a very tall horse, chalk-white and powerfully built. When I say he was tall, by the way, I mean it; Kamthaka was twenty-five feet tall, an unusually massive horse and consequently very heavy. (ASV 5:3; NK) How would father's guards not hear his mighty hoofbeats, especially because, as I said, he was covered with little tinkly bronze bells? That wasn't going to be particularly helpful, I now realized. Still, I left them on him because they looked absolutely charming.

I mounted Kamthaka and stroked his mighty head, then leaned forward and whispered in his ear, "Your speed and energy will now help save the world, excellent steed!" A few moments later we went forth, me on Kamthaka's back, Chandaka holding onto Kamthaka's tail and being pulled behind. (ASV 5:78; NK) We stole quietly through the palace grounds, trying to avoid guards, me putting them to sleep when necessary. Luckily for us, the gods essentially "silenced" Kamthaka's hoofbeats by placing their hands under his mighty hooves every step he took. (ASV 5:81)

Reaching the main gate, we stopped. It was not only closed but also extremely heavy; it would take a thousand men to open this gate. While I was as strong as a *billion elephants* (NK), I wasn't in the mood to use my brute strength to open the gate. Instead, I remember thinking to myself, "If I cannot magically open this gate, I will have Kamthaka jump over it!" Kamthaka was apparently thinking along the same lines. "If this gate does not magically open, I will leap over it with my master on my back and Chandaka holding onto my tail!" Chandaka was thinking more or less exactly the same thing: "If this gate does not magically open, I will *personally* leap over it with my master on my shoulder and Kamthaka under my arm!" (NK) When I heard about Chandaka's claim, I shook my head, slightly piqued. "First of all, I'm not the size of a parrot," I remember thinking. "I couldn't possibly ride on Chandaka's shoulder. Second of all, Kamthaka is not the size of a house cat—he couldn't fit under Chandaka's arm!" It turns out none of these things were necessary, however, because the God of the Gate (and no, I hadn't realized there *was* a God of the Gate, but there was and he turned out to be a very nice man) simply opened the gate for us and allowed us to exit the palace grounds that way. (NK)

It was at that moment that Mara, the god of death and delusion, first appeared to me. He manifested in the sky above me—he was tall, with a thick black moustache—and commanded me to turn back. "Stay at your father's palace, young prince," Mara hissed down at me. "If you do so, you will rule the entire *world*!" As this was the first time I had ever met Mara, I looked up and asked, "Who are you?" "I am Vasavatti," Mara replied. (The truth was that he was *from* Vasavatti, so I'm not sure why he said he *was* Vasavatti, other than he was trying to confuse me, which he usually was.) Now that I understood who Mara was, I nodded coolly and announced, "I do not wish to be a king, rather I wish to be a *savior*." Mara glared down at me for a moment, then snarled, "Every bad thought you ever have, young prince, *I will know about*." (NK) Suddenly he was gone—then, just as suddenly, he was right next to me, invisible, but definitely present, watching over me and waiting. I found this slightly disconcerting; I won't deny that it rattled me a little. It turned out, however, that "I am watching over you all the time" was Mara's high-water mark of scariness. Everything he said and did from that moment on was, as you will see, breathtakingly feeble.

Outside the palace walls, I stopped and looked back. "Farewell, old life," I cried out. "Farewell luxury, farewell privilege and indulgence, yes, farewell!" With that, I pulled off all of my jewelry. (ASV 6:12–13) (I was wearing rings, bracelets, earrings and toe-rings, not to mention my small tiara.) Before we left, Chandaka had draped a turban around my head filled with a thousand (or possibly ten thousand) layers of jewels and gems, which made my head look like a gigantic flower. (NK) I then stripped off my silken clothes. A monk passed by and I yelled over at him. "You there! Throw me your clothes! I cannot be a holy man while wearing silks!" (This monk turned out to be, no surprise at all, a god.) (NK)

"Hold up my mirror," I commanded of Chandaka. Seeing my reflection in the bronze, I inhaled sharply, strangely moved by what I beheld. "I look so . . . *holy*," I murmured to myself. Only one thing was wrong with the picture. Reaching up with one hand, I grabbed my long, luxurious hair. "No, my lord," Chandaka whispered. "Not your magnificent hair." "Yes, Chandaka, YES." I yanked up my hair and diadem (the sort of mini-tiara I was wearing) and bellowed, "Who is fit to cut a bodhisattva's hair? *No one!*" With that, I chopped my hair off and threw it, along with my diadem, straight up into the air. (ASV 6:57) "If I am to become a Buddha, let my hair and mini-tiara float in mid-air!" I proclaimed. "If not, let them fall to the ground!" I was confident that my hair and mini-tiara *would* float in mid-air obviously. I wouldn't have made that statement otherwise. Still, I was slightly relieved to see my hair and mini-tiara floating in mid-air before me. (NK) (I later learned that the god Sakka—who had one thousand eyes, by the way—had sucked my hair and mini-tiara up to heaven, placed them in a jewel box and built a shrine to them.) (ASV 6:58) (I *was* Sakka in thirty-six different lifetimes, incidentally.) (ITI 12)

I crossed to Kamthaka and stared him in the eye. "You have served me well, gallant steed. I grieve at our imminent separation, but sadly, the time has come. You are an excellent horse and I promise that you will have an excellent rebirth! At the very least, the *very* least, Kamthaka, you will not go to hell. Is that a tear streaming down your face, noble friend? It is, and I know why you cry too, for I know what you are thinking: 'Do not go, dear prince, for you are indeed my hero.' Yet go I must, dear Kamthaka." At this, Kamthaka burst into copious tears. (ASV 6:57) I held my webbed hand up to his face and spoke tenderly, "Be brave, dear Kamthaka, you must be brave." "But how will I live with the grief of never seeing you again, master?" I saw in Kamthaka's eyes. "You will be fine, my friend," I started to say, but before I could get the words out, Kamthaka suddenly keeled over dead. He had died of a broken heart! (NK)

I turned away from Kamthaka's corpse and glanced over at Chandaka. "In time, friend charioteer, my leaving the palace this night will come to be known as the 'Great Going Forth.'"

"Excellent, my lord."

"It is now time for me to begin attaining immortality, Chandaka. Farewell!" With that, feeling full of confidence and vigor, I strode manfully into the forest. "I look like the peak of a golden mountain," I remember thinking to myself as I walked. "Or maybe more like a cross between a cloud and an elephant. Or possibly a lion and the moon—or some mix of those things in any case." (ASV 5:26)

It was a dark night; consequently, it was quite helpful when some gods appeared and lit torches for me—a lot of torches, actually—a quarter of a million, to be precise. Less helpful but still nice was the way millions of musical instruments floated around me, playing songs in my honor as I walked. (NK) Not helpful in the least, frankly, was the way some bird-like gods sprinkled perfume and powder down on me. These bird-gods dumped so much perfume and powder on me that before long the trail was nothing but a thick, gloppy mess. Still, the bird-gods wouldn't stop. I finally decided the only way to get them to quit what they were doing was to stop walking, which I did. "What I have done this night is the single boldest step any human has *ever* taken," I announced loudly. "I do it not for my own sake but for the sake of all humanity, so that they might not suffer!

HEAR ME NOW, UNIVERSE, OH HEAR ME, *I WILL NOW BEGIN TO CURE YOU!*"

६

Somewhat strangely, it took me six years to actually discover the cure. Even in hindsight, I'm still not quite sure why things took so long. I already knew that life was suffering. I'd known that since the awful "Four Sights" day with Chandaka, when I'd first grasped that sickness, old age and death were parts of human existence. I also already knew by this time that all suffering stemmed from desire; that was the reason I had left Father's palace and renounced all of my worldly goods. I *further* knew that the only way to escape suffering was to escape desire. What I did not yet know was *how* to escape desire. *Could* one escape desire, I sometimes wondered to myself? It seemed "built-in" to human nature. Could it *actually* be overcome? Years passed with no answer to this question.

It's not that I wasn't *searching* for the answer; I definitely was. I became a *"shamana,"* a seeker of the truth. I wandered far and wide across the Ganges Plain, searching for wise men who I felt could help me find the truth. The gurus Alara Kalama and Ramaputta, between them, taught me to meditate. I was instantly gifted at meditation; literally no one had ever been as good at meditation as me before; people would come from miles around just to watch me meditate, dazzled by the extremely rarefied states of *"jhana"* (concentration) which I regularly achieved. (AP 1:160–167) Again, I say this not out of "ego," because, again,

I *have* no "ego;" it is simply the case that I was a meditation "prodigy."

Alara Kalama and Ramaputta each asked me to continue on with them. "You are a meditating *genius,* Siddhartha," they both said to me. "Won't you please take over for me?" In both cases I demurred; I was not yet ready to be a teacher because I had not yet found the *answer.* "Life is pain," my mind repeated over and over again. "But how to *escape* the pain?"

After leaving my two teachers, I went back to the forest and spent the next several years living with five other ascetics, Kondanna being the oldest and wisest of them. (Kondanna had actually been one of the seers who my father had brought in to predict my future when I was a baby—the only one who had predicted *correctly*, in fact.) (NK) The six of us spent our time trying to burn off bad "*karma*." More on *karma* later, but the gist of it is this: You get what you deserve in this world. If you are sick, poor, crippled, ugly, stupid—well, you deserve that. If, on the other hand, you are a rich, handsome genius-prince—well, you deserve that too. (SK; SAL)

The five ascetics and I all believed that the way to eliminate bad *karma* was to suffer as much as possible in this lifetime so that we might suffer less in the next lifetime. An annoying question did occur to me once or twice during this difficult stretch: "If I am suffering *this* badly, does that mean that I 'deserve' it?" The answer to this question, however, was obvious: I was *choosing* to suffer and that was totally different.

The five ascetics and I practiced extreme self-denial. Our goal was to overcome our physical body, to free ourselves from hunger, from "appetites" of all kinds, in fact. Sometimes I ate nothing but rocks for days; other times I ate air, yet other times I ate cow manure. A few times I ate my own feces. (ASV 7:15–16; MJ 12) I remember thinking at one point, "What if I stopped eating entirely?" Immediately afterwards, however, some gods appeared before me and said, "Please, sir, do not cut off your food intake. If you do, we will have no choice but to inject food directly into your pores." "Into my *pores?*" I replied. "How is that even *possible? My* pores aren't the size of little *mouths!*" "Nevertheless, we will absolutely do it, sir." (NK; MJ 12; MH 1:240–49) So I kept eating.

Sometimes I slept on thorns; other times I slept on the sharpest, pointiest rocks I could find. One time, I found a dead body and used its skull as my pillow. One morning I remember waking up feeling what I thought was warm rainwater sprinkling down on me, but when I opened my eyes it turned out to be some local boys urinating on my head. Afterwards the largest and most aggressive boy jammed two sticks in my ears and dangled me around like a puppet. (MJ 12) (I probably weighed all of seventy pounds by this time.) It was deeply humiliating. I remember pressing lightly on my stomach one day and thinking, "I can feel my *spine.* You're not supposed to be able to feel your spine when you touch your stomach." I remember stroking my hair not long after that and it instantly starting to fall out in dull, ragged clumps in my hand.

Years passed this way. I was thirty-three . . . then thirty-four . . . then thirty-five years old. My health began to falter. My skin dried up; I started to look like a piece of dried fruit. "There *must* be a better way of finding the truth," I remember thinking to myself on one particularly uncomfortable day. "Starving myself cannot *possibly* be the path to enlightenment. I am literally destroying myself here and I don't understand anything more about how to escape suffering than I did when I started." I felt like I'd been beating my head against a wall for a very long time by this point.

One day I became so frail and exhausted that I fell face forward into a pile of my own excrement. (MH 1:240–49) I remember rising wobbly from my squat and looking down at the small brown pile, and at that point I must have blacked out because my next memory is waking up with my face half-buried in my own feces. As I lay there, semi-conscious, I heard the gods whispering worriedly about me. "He's *dead,*" one of them said.

"No no, he's only *resting*," replied another. (Why he thought I would rest facedown in a pile of my own shit, I do not know. One of these gods even went to my father and told him I was dead. "I don't believe you," Father instantly replied and not long afterwards the god had to return and admit, "Actually, he's fine.") (NK) Then I heard a third voice, thin and girlish, right next to me. "Are you alright, sir?" the voice asked.

I turned and looked up. "Sojata" (for that was the child's name) gazed down at me, a concerned look on her sweet young face. "I fell face-forward into my own feces, child," I whispered.

"You need food, sir, you are quite thin. Would you like some rice porridge?" I stared at the child, uncomprehending. "You must *eat*, sir," she repeated.

My mind was feverish, disoriented. Rice porridge? How could I possibly eat that? I was an *ascetic*, devoted to suffering and self-abnegation. How could I indulge myself with milk and honey-infused porridge?

Sojata gently helped me to sit up and tenderly wiped the feces off my face with a rag. She removed a small wooden bowl from her basket and, kneeling next to me, dipped a spoon into the bowl and lifted the rice porridge to my mouth. "I cannot, child," I whispered. "I have vowed to *suffer*."

"Eat, sir," the child said, tenderly touching the spoon to my lips.

"I will not open my mouth," I thought to myself. "I will not, I will *not*, I will—" I opened my mouth and ate the porridge. It was warm, sweet, soft—almost indescribably delicious. I swallowed and opened my mouth again. Sojata refilled the spoon and fed me. Then she did it again—and again—and again.

Five minutes later the small wooden bowl was empty and Sojata, with a sweet, shy smile, turned and headed home. (MH 1:240–49)

"That little girl just saved my life," I thought to myself as I watched her depart. "Someday I must find a way to repay not only *her* but her entire *sex*." (I never did so because before long

I realized that women were all dangerous crocodiles who should be avoided as much as humanly possible, but at that moment I did think it.)

After eating the rice porridge, I quickly felt more clear-headed. "What I've been doing has been *madness*," I remember thinking. "Humans cannot live on rocks or their own feces—humans are meant to eat normally, like animals do. If you saw a tiger that only ate rocks or its own feces, you would think to yourself, 'That is an insane tiger.'" Extreme asceticism was *not* the path to enlightenment, I now understood. I began to eat normally again and before long I didn't look like a fleshtone-painted skeleton anymore.

When I rejoined my five ascetic friends, they were instantly appalled at the change that had come over me. "What have you *done*, Gotama?" Kondanna asked in a hushed, disbelieving voice as I approached them.

I told him the truth. "To start with, Kondanna, I ate some rice porridge."

"*Rice porridge*," Kondanna sputtered, as if these two words constituted the worst obscenity imaginable. The other ascetics shook their heads in horror.

"I feel better now that I am eating normally, friends," I continued. "My mind is much clearer."

"You are no longer an ascetic, Gotama," Kondanna announced firmly. "You have broken the ascetic vow and therefore we want nothing more to do with you."

"Kondanna, listen to me, there is another way, a better way, a *middle way*."

But Kondanna wouldn't listen. With a small dismissive wave of his hand, he and the others turned and hurried away from me. (At least as much as men who weigh sixty-five pounds can be said to "hurry," that is. They "speed-hobbled" away from me is perhaps a more accurate description.) After they were all gone I stood for a moment in silence. "What next?" I remember asking myself.

Suddenly a fully formed thought popped into my mind: "*The moment has arrived, Gotama.*"

"What?" I remember speaking aloud.

"*You have been asleep. Now it is time to **wake up**,*" my mind proclaimed.

7

An hour later I sat down under a large tree and announced to myself, "I will not move from this place, nor will I urinate or defecate, until I have achieved my goal of *defeating death*!" (NK; ASV 12:118) In heaven, the gods burst into applause upon hearing that. One god, however, was not pleased that I was on the verge of, shall we say, "piercing the veil." That god was Mara, the god of death and delusion, my old nemesis. "Why do you look so upset, Father?" his three daughters, Lust, Delight and Appetite, asked him. "This sage Siddhartha is about to conquer my realm, daughters!" Mara cried. "If he succeeds, my rule will come to an end!" (ASV 13:15) (Given that Mara's "realm" was death and that the *desirability* of death was what I was just about to grasp, I've never really understood why he was trying to stop me; weren't we basically on the same team?) "Before this sage's vision is realized," Mara continued to his daughters, "we must fly down to earth and STOP HIM!" (NK)

A bit later, the four of them landed directly in front of me. Mara, not wasting any time, instantly aimed his bow and arrow at me. "Rise, sage!" he demanded. "Abandon your search immediately or I will shoot you with this love-tipped arrow! Rise, I said—RISE!!" I sat motionless, my hands gently folded before me, my eyes lightly closed. When Mara shot his love-tipped arrow at me, I did not even flinch. Seeing that, Mara slowly sank to the ground and muttered to himself, "The sage does not even notice the arrow I shot him with, does he have no *feelings?*" Suddenly his face darkened with rage. "He is not even *worthy* of my arrows, nor of the temptations of my three lovely daughters!" (Who were not, by the way, all that lovely. Lust was pudgy, with a moon-face; Appetite was bony, with an oversized nose; Desire had bad teeth and was slightly cross-eyed.) "What he deserves is to be destroyed!! DEMONS, ATTACK!!" Mara now shrieked and in an instant I was surrounded by demons waving clubs, swords and (weirdly, I thought) trees at me. (ASV 13:14–18)

These demons were hideous-looking creatures. There were three-headed fish with spotted bellies and one-eyed horses with elephant ears. There were cat-faced demons with messy, unkempt hair (sickening) and goat-faced demons who were balding (even *more* sickening.) Many of the demons were nude. They all hopped around in front of me, trying to scare me. But I sat motionless, calm in the face of the storm. "*Terrify him, you fools!*" Mara screamed at his demons and now they all stopped dancing around and started making scary faces at me, rapidly opening and closing their mouths and bugging their eyes out. One of the demons (a three-headed goat with messy hair) rolled his eyes around in his head and raised a heavy club as if he was going to bash me. Instantly I paralyzed him with love, however, and he stood there frozen, club in mid-air, blinking in confusion. A female demon named "Megahali" (and why I knew her name I'm still not exactly sure; none of the other demons even had names to my knowledge, but "Megahali" definitely did) grabbed a skull and started gyrating around with it in front of me. I'm not sure what she was trying to achieve, kind of a mix of "scary" and "sexy," I guess, but when I ignored her, she had to slink away ignominiously. (ASV 13:49)

At that moment, a god bellowed down from the sky: "Give up, Mara! Your attempts to stop this sage are ignoble and your greatness is being compromised by your pride!" (ASV 13:69)

I liked everything about what this god said except for that last bit about Mara's "greatness." Mara was *not* great; Mara was an impotent, blustery fool. In any case, the gods' words only seemed to inflame Mara, who now marched on me with an Army of Demons which was mind-bogglingly huge, like literally extending to the edge of the *universe*. Mara was now riding on a 50,000-foot-tall elephant named "Girimikhala." (How he got onto a 50,000-foot-tall elephant, I'm still not sure.)

As all this was happening, the gods gathered in heaven to gaze down on the battle. They started singing fight-songs to me, led by a giant snake named Makahala. This was going to be a rout and the gods all knew it: An army of demons the size of the entire universe led by a devil-king riding a ten-mile-tall elephant versus one man, sitting quietly under a tree. *No contest*. As Mara's army drew nearer to me, however, for some unknown reason the gods all suddenly panicked and began to sprint away in every direction. (NK) You'd have thought that scaring the gods this way would have given Mara a boost of confidence, but it definitely didn't. "Men," he suddenly called out to his giant army, "we cannot possibly defeat this sage in a fair fight. Let us therefore attack him from *behind*!"

Mara created a massive tornado and flung it at me. Gale-force winds, powerful enough to blow mountains to pieces, rumbled towards me. My majesty was so profound, however, that the winds calmed before me, in the end not even stirring the hem of my garment. Next Mara tried to drown me, causing a sudden massive downpour, so much rain that it literally hollowed the earth out. Almost instantly the water all around me was a hundred feet high. Like the wind, however, the rain quickly receded before my virtuousness and in the end did not even dampen the hem of my garment. I could tell that Mara was getting frustrated now. He picked up a bunch of mountains (I *think* they were volcanoes—they were definitely fiery) and flung them at me. Before my bottomless goodness, however, the volcanoes turned to flowers. Shaking his head in disbelief, Mara hurled swords, daggers, darts and spears at me. Once again, I turned them to flowers. Cursing now, Mara threw a bunch of burning coal at me; needless to say, I turned it into flowers. (NK)

Mara's next move was a sandstorm. "He's getting desperate," I remember thinking to myself. "If fiery mountains didn't scare me, I'm not sure why he thinks a *sandstorm* is going to." I quickly turned the sand into (what else?) flowers. Then Mara tried mud. "Mud?" I remember musing. "Mara thinks he can destroy me with mud?" To be fair, it was *flaming* mud, which was slightly disconcerting because, well, it didn't make sense to me. "How can 'flaming mud' even exist?" I remember thinking. "It's an oxymoron." No matter though, I turned the flaming mud into sweet-smelling ointments.

Mara's last move was fog, which I felt was frankly embarrassing because how do you kill someone with fog? "Mara's sense of rhythm is atrocious," I remember thinking at the time. "He should have *started* with fog, then built up to volcanos, not vice versa." Finally, sputtering with rage, Mara charged me on his giant elephant and screamed, "Get up from under that Bodhi tree, sage, that is MY spot!" This comment irked me. For the first time, I opened my eyes and looked straight back at him. "You are sadly mistaken, Mara, this spot is *not* yours, this spot is *mine.*" His eyes flashing with fury, Mara hurled a razor-edged disc at my head. Did he not realize by this time that I would instantly turn it into flowers, which would then hover prettily over my head? If he didn't, he should have, because that is exactly what I did. In heaven, where the gods had by now regathered after previously running away, they all craned their necks for a better view and someone cried out, "Has Siddhartha's handsome body been harmed?" Of course it hadn't been harmed in the least and I honestly have no idea why they thought that. (NK)

At that point I pointed down at the earth and demanded, "Are you or are you not my witness?" and the earth responded with a giant series of echoes, as if to say, "I AM your witness, Exalted One!" That seemed to do it. Hearing these mighty echoes, Mara's demons sprinted off in a tizzy, some of them stripping off their clothes and shrieking in terror as they dashed away. The cheer "Mara is defeated, Siddhartha has triumphed, let us now serenade him!" went up in heaven. Shortly thereafter, a bunch of gods marched towards my tree, singing, "Hooray for the illustrious Buddha! Farewell to the evil Mara!" They all threw flowers at me but honestly, flowers were about the *last* thing I needed at that point, I was half-buried in flowers. A few of them dumped fancy powders and ointments on me, which I liked a bit better. Some of the gods waved banners reading, "HOORAY FOR THE BUDDHA!" which I did like. Overall, it was a moment of unlimited glory and splendor, never to be forgotten. (NK)

ड

After the gods departed, I sat in silence for a long moment, unsure what would happen next. Then, in a flash, and for the very first time, I remembered all of my previous lifetimes, stretching backwards over many "*kalpas*." (ASV 14:4) What is a *kalpa*, you ask? Imagine an enormous, rocky mountain. Now imagine a small bird landing on that rocky mountain once every hundred years with silk shoes on its tiny little feet. A *kalpa* is how long it would take that little bird to wear that rocky mountain down to nothing with its silk shoes. (SY 15:5) This is to say that a *kalpa* is essentially "infinity." I will refer to other significant past lives later in my story but for now it will suffice to describe the following highly meaningful one.

Once I had been a rabbit. Not just any rabbit, though; I had been a marvelously strong, kind and wise rabbit. I was so wise, in fact, that all the other animals in the forest elected me as their king. I was also such a magnanimous rabbit that I literally sacrificed my life simply so that I might be eaten. (The moment I decided to sacrifice myself, by the way, three things happened: (1) There was a massive earthquake; (2) Heavenly music played; (3) I was showered with pollen.)

After I made the decision to sacrifice myself, I instantly hopped into Brahma's fire and cooked myself. Did the flames hurt? No, they did not, they felt cool and refreshing, in fact. After

I was cooked, Brahma escorted me up to heaven. (Brahma's hands, for those who are curious, were milky-white, very soft and covered with rings; they were, in short, exquisite.) In heaven, Brahma informed the other gods of my profound sacrifice, built some statues of me and then, rather remarkably, drew a picture of me on the moon! This drawing of rabbit-me on the moon is, in some sense, one of the great wonders of the universe. Anyway, that's the kind of being I was, a rabbit who ends up with his image on the moon because of his vast generosity and bottomless compassion. (I don't remember, by the way, whether Brahma actually ate me, but I think he did and I presume that I tasted utterly delicious.) (HJAT)

At that moment, after all my endless searching, awakening finally occurred. Like a flash of lightning, insight came. (ANG 5:146) Life was pain . . . of *course* life was pain . . . and there was literally no way to avoid that pain . . . except *one*.

Stop life. (ASV 14:56; SY 12:65) "For where there is no life," I whispered to myself, "there can be no *death*!" By undoing the cord, I suddenly grasped, one could achieve the true goal of existence: <u>Non</u>-existence.

The final veils of ignorance dropped away at that moment. I knew Absolute Truth. There was nothing, literally nothing, that I did not understand at that moment. I grasped everything that had happened in the past, everything that would happen in the future and everything that was happening at that moment. Some people have said that I "woke up" in that moment and I think that is a fair way of putting it. I had been asleep and now I awoke. (ASV 14:66–68; ITI 112)

"Dump more flowers on him!" I heard a god yell, which was followed by another god yelling, "No, *don't* dump more flowers on him—there's no reason for it!" I thought this second remark was rude, because there definitely was reason for dumping flowers on me, I had just attained Absolute Knowledge, after all! On the other hand, I was glad not to have more flowers dumped on me; I was getting pretty sick of it by that point.

Suddenly I was lifted a hundred feet in the air. Glancing down, I noticed that I was sitting on a throne. I yelled up at the gods, wanting to get their attention. *"Ho!"* I cried up to them. "I have attained perfect knowledge, I am pure-hearted and wise, the destroyer of all pain, HO, I AM THE BUDDHA!" The gods dumped a bunch of flowers on me and my throne was lowered back to the ground. "What exactly was the point of *that*?" I remember wondering to myself. (ASV 14:70–76)

"He is like a cloud," I heard one god say about me. "No, he is like a *thunderbolt* with a hundred edges," another god offered. "I think he is like a gem," a third god insisted, followed by: "a tree," "a jar" and "a cow." "They should have stopped with saying I was like a thunderbolt with a hundred edges," I remember thinking. "Because I'm not like a jar and I am nothing like a cow." (ASV 14:80–84)

At that point, the giant snake Makahala showed up and wrapped me in his coils, apparently believing he was protecting me from gnats. (MV 1:3) I tried to tell him to let me go, that I had been enlightened and needed to save the world, but he was squeezing me so tightly that I couldn't even make a sound. He held me like that for a week, until the gods then started pouring jugs of water over us and he slithered away.

After that, who should come shambling up to me but Mara, once again accompanied by his three daughters. "You've accomplished your goals, sage, why don't you go straight to *nirvana*?" Mara asked me, apparently thinking he was being clever. "First I must save the world," I replied and Mara shrieked and ran away. (SY 4:1) (My *god*, he was feeble.) His daughters, however, remained behind and started trying to seduce me. Appetite, with her long, bony face, whispered, "I am Appetite, sage, worship me or I will *hug the life out of you*." She tried to hug me but I side-stepped her a few times until she eventually gave up and trudged away. Then Delight, who had a shrill, nasal voice, droned, "I am Delight and I offer you delight, sage, bringing within your reach . . . *delight*." Did she feel embarrassed to have used her own name three times in one sentence? I don't know, but she definitely should have. When I didn't respond to Delight, she started cursing at me and stormed away. (ASV 15:13–22)

Off a look from Lust, Mara's three daughters stepped a few feet away from me and conferred in low voices. A moment later they returned, having given themselves "make-overs," looking slightly better than they had previously. ("I'm not sure why they didn't start *off* looking that way," I remember thinking to myself.) "Dear Tathagata," they said to me in unison ("Tathagata" was my new moniker, by the way, it meant "Perfect One," because that's what I now was), "*please* allow us to be your devoted followers." When I ignored them, they transformed themselves yet again, this time into three old crones. "We are old, sir, pitiful and terrified of death, *please* help us," they croaked. This request I agreed to and before long Mara's daughters were worshipping me. (ASV 15:30–36)

Mara himself, shameless creature that he was, took one last shot at me. "I knew you would become a Buddha!" he yelled down from heaven. "By my actions today, I have *helped* you!"

"You have *lost*, Mara" I responded. "Now *go away*."

"I am defeated," Mara muttered in a maudlin tone of voice and in a flash he was gone, as were his daughters.

Alone under the Bodhi tree, a question popped into my mind: Did I *actually* want to share these profound insights with the world? Given how irrationally attached to life most humans were, given how many of them actually *enjoyed* life, even took pleasure in it (or *thought* they did anyway), what would be the point of speaking to them? How could such limited creatures *ever* grasp my stupendous insights? "Perhaps I will just stay here under the Bodhi tree and wait for my blissful extinction," I remember thinking. (SY 6:1)

At that moment Brahma appeared before me, a vision of white and gold, his splendid, silky robe hanging elegantly off one shoulder, his white parasol propped casually on the other shoulder. "Brahma?" I whispered. "What are *you* doing here?"

"Perfect One," Brahma replied. "You *must* teach the world of your magnificent insights, for if you do not the world itself will *die*."

When I remained silent, Brahma continued. "You are correct that there are many who will *not* understand your words, Sublime One."

"Yes."

"But there are some, a few, who *will* understand you, Stainless One." (I wasn't sure I liked that nickname very much, by the way; "Who ever said I was 'stained'?" crossed my mind.) "Only *you* can help mankind, Perfect One," Brahma implored me. "Arise, victorious hero! Arise and SAVE THE WORLD!"

When I finally rose to my feet, Brahma yelled, "The Blessed One has agreed!" and instantly disappeared. (AP 1:167–73; MV 1:5)

I looked around, noticing that my mind was purified. "I will be like a pinprick, popping the bubbles of ignorance and delusion, revealing their utter emptiness," I thought to myself. "Where there is ignorance, I will inform. Where there is darkness, I will enlighten. And where there is conflict, I will bring *love*."

part 2: middle

৯

After I had walked some distance towards the nearest town, I met an ascetic named Upana the Ajivaka on the road. I smiled broadly at him; my joy must have been palpable. Upana looked at me and cocked his head slightly. "You look well, my friend," he said. "Tell me, who is your teacher?" I was in such excellent spirits that I decided to respond to him in a kind of poem:

I am the one who's transcended all pain.
I am the knower, I'll say it again.
I have renounced all the world can give
I am the one who now knows how to LIVE!

When Upana stared at me blankly, I continued.

I am a one-of-a-kind, that is true
No one can match me; oh please tell me who?
Even the gods know that I am their better
I am released now and I have no fetter!

When Upana still stared at me in silence, I raised my voice a little and continued with my poem.

I am the king of the whole universe

I am the teacher and I am the nurse
I am Perfection, Enlightenment, Truth
I am exalted, I tell you forsooth!

Upana finally nodded slightly and said, "You are very confident, sir."

"Wrong!" I instantly cried. "I am not 'confident' in the least! What I am is **victorious!**"

"Well, good luck," Upana the Ajivaka said and walked away. As I watched him depart I shook my head sadly, knowing that he would be *karmically* punished for his rank disrespect towards me. (And also for walking around nude because I forgot to mention that "Ajivaka" means "nude.") (AP 1:167–73)

As I continued walking, a question entered my mind: "Who should I teach *first*?" Instantly I knew the answer. "Of course," I thought, "I will go see my old teacher, Alara Kalama! Alara Kalama is a wise and thoughtful man, he sees things clearly, he is the perfect person!" Feeling excited, I started off towards where Alara Kalama lived, but I hadn't traveled very far when a god (I didn't know his name; he was youngish, with a hangdog face and lank hair) appeared before me. "Excuse me, sir," the god drawled, "but your old friend, Alara Kalama?"

"Yes?" I quickly replied.

"He's dead."

"WHAT? Alara Kalama is *dead?* When?"

"Seven days ago."

"But this is terrible, Alara Kalama was to have been my first student!"

"Yes, well, as I said, he's dead." The god stared at me with a dull look on his long face for a moment, then turned and strolled away. I stood there after he left, trying to decide who to teach now. Then it hit me: "My *other* old teacher, Ramaputta!" I cried aloud. "Like Alara Kalama, Ramaputta is a wise and thoughtful man. He sees things clearly. He will certainly understand my teachings. Ramaputta is the perfect person!" Filled with renewed excitement, I started towards where Ramaputta lived, but after a few steps that same lank-haired young god appeared before me again.

"Excuse me, sir."

"What is it now?"

"Your other old teacher, Ramaputta?"

"Yes, *yes*?"

"He's dead too."

"What?? When?"

"Um . . . last night, I think?"

"Ramaputta died *last night*?? Of what?"

"I don't know that, sir, I just know that he's dead."

"But this is terrible. I was on my way to teach him!"

"Yes, well, as I said, he's dead. Anyway, goodbye, sir." (MV 1:6; AP 1:163–72)

The young god slouched away and I stood there, once again uncertain. "*Now* who should I teach?" I asked myself. "Alara Kalama and Ramaputta are both dead. Who else is there?" I stroked my chin for a long moment, then suddenly knew the answer. "Of course!" I thought. "Kondanna and the other ascetics! I have spent a great deal of time with them over the past few years. They are the perfect ones to start with!"

The last time I'd seen Kondanna and the other ascetics had been several months earlier, not long after I'd eaten the rice porridge Sujata had given me. They had openly scorned me at that time. Now, as I strode back towards them, they instantly started mocking me. "Look who's here, friends, it's none other than Prince Siddhartha."

"Looking for some milk and honey, Prince Siddhartha?"

"Looking for a cushion to sit on?"

"Looking for—?"

Suddenly they all stopped and fell silent, stunned by the radiance of my visage. Almost as if against their own wills, the ascetics all leapt to their feet and bowed deeply to me. "Friend," several of them murmured. "*Friend.*" (ASV 15:108; MV 1:6) I stopped and looked at them, steely-eyed. "First of all, do not call me 'friend' again," I said. "I am now a Perfectly Enlightened Being, a Buddha, and I am here to teach you."

Kondanna shook his head, incredulous. "On what basis do you claim to have achieved such god-like status, Gotama?" he stammered.

"I have *awakened*, Kondanna. I have found the solution to suffering. And while I do not care for *myself* whether you treat me with the proper respect, for I have transcended ego, it is not, in a larger sense, permissible to refer to a Buddha as 'friend.'" (AP 1:167–73; DP 153–54)

"What *should* we call you then?"

"You may call me 'Tathagata.'"

" . . . Perfect One?"

"Correct. You may also call me 'Exalted One,' 'Insightful One' or 'Gifted One.' 'The Essence of Perfection' is acceptable too, as is 'Leader of the Caravan,' 'Taster of Truth' and 'Lord of the World.'" (ASV 16:70–74)

The ascetics stared at me, dumbfounded. "Many great and venerable thinkers have come before you, Gotama. None of them has ever claimed the kind of supreme enlightenment you are claiming," one said. "On what basis do you do so when you are still so young?"

"Tell me, *bikkhu*," I shot back, "do you doubt *fire* when it is young?" They all stared at me, startled by my astonishing question. "Monks," I continued, looking them in the eye one by one, "have you ever heard me speak this way before?" (Samy. 3:1)

"No, Gotama," they all murmured. "Never."

"I tell you that I have understood the nature of *Absolute Reality* and I am here to teach it to you if you wish to learn. Do you wish to learn?"

One by one, each of them slowly nodded.

"Excellent," I said, then spread my arms widely and called out in a loud, clear voice: "The Great Wheel of Truth will now begin to turn!"

ा॑ठ

The following day the ascetics sat before me. "To begin with, *bikkhus,* there are the Four Noble Truths. Noble Truth Number One: Life is pain."

I saw slight disappointment in their eyes: "We obviously already *knew* that, Gotama," I could imagine they were thinking.

"Noble Truth Number Two:" I continued. "All suffering comes from *desire.*" I saw more disappointment in their eyes. "We understood that already too, Gotama. That's why we're starving ourselves out here, because we're trying to overcome our desires."

"Noble Truth Number Three:" I went on, lowering my voice solemnly. "The suffering that stems from desire can be ended."

Oh, that one got their attention. Kondanna suddenly sat forward and stared at me intently. "But how, Tathagata?"

"That, Kondanna, is Noble Truth Number Four. Are you ready to hear it?"

"Yes, *of course!*"

"Noble Truth Number Four: All that is required to end desire . . ." I paused meaningfully: "Is the following *eight* things." (SY 45:8)

"I'm sorry . . . Did you not just say there were Four Noble Truths, Tathagata?"

"I did, Kondanna."

"Is it not eleven now?"

"No, Kondanna, it is four. It is simply that Noble Truth Number Four has eight *parts* to it, that's all."

"It kind of *is* eleven then," I heard another ascetic mutter under his breath.

"No, *bikkhu,* it is NOT eleven," I replied sharply. "It is *four*. Noble Truth Number Four has eight *parts* to it but that does not change the fact that there are Four Noble Truths."

"What *are* the eight parts to Noble Truth Number Four, Tathagata?" Kondanna asked.

"Thank you for asking, Kondanna. The answer is simple. In order to fulfill Noble Truth Number Four and overcome desire, one must do the following eight things: (1) Have the right views; (2) Have the right intentions; (3) Speak the right words; (4) Perform the right actions; (5) Do the right work; (6) Make the right effort; (7) Have the right state of mind and (8) Practice the right concentration."

There was a lengthy pause, then one of the ascetics said in a small voice, "That actually sounds rather difficult, Tathagata."

"No, it is quite easy, you will see."

Kondanna, who had been staring thoughtfully at the ground, suddenly looked up at me, a glimmer of understanding in his eyes. "Are you suggesting, Tathagata, that by following the eight steps of Noble Truth Number Four we might, in time, *actually* overcome desire?"

"That is exactly what I am suggesting, Kondanna."

Kondanna continued, his eyes wide and amazed. "And that by overcoming desire, we might achieve *nirvana?*"

"Kondanna has understood, *bikkhus,*" I announced. "Kondanna has *understood.*" (After that day, I gave Kondanna the nickname "Anna Kondanna," which means "Kondanna has understood." It was literal, I grant you, but it was definitely accurate.) At the moment of Kondanna's spiritual awakening, the gods cheered happily. "The *dharma* wheel has been set in motion and cannot be stopped by anyone on earth!" they all shouted in celebration. It was apparently quite exciting. (DCP 420–24)

The following day, we regathered. "I spoke to you yesterday of the Noble Eightfold Path, *bikkhus*. Today I will more fully explain it. Some questions for you: When the Tathagata says 'Right View,' what does he mean by that? Answer: When the Tathagata says 'Right View,' what he means is knowledge of his words. What does the Tathagata mean by 'Right Intention'? 'Right Intention' is the intention to follow the Tathagata's words. What does he mean by 'Right Speech'? 'Right Speech' means not denying the truth of the Tathagata's words."

"Does every step on the Eightfold Path involve nothing more than obeying your words, Tathagata?"

"No, Vappa, the Eightfold Path is far larger and more profound than that. Regarding Right Speech, for instance, it also means don't speak of trivial things, like clothing or criminals; it means be, you know, *lovable*. (DG 22; MJ 41) Moving on, step number four on the Noble Eightfold Path is *Right Action*. There are five specific components to Right Action."

"Aren't we sort of up to sixteen now?" I heard one of the ascetics whisper, but I ignored that. "The first rule of Right Action is to not have sex. Sex is very bad, *bikkhus*, terrible really. It is embarrassing and messy, but more than that sex leads to children who are nothing but fetters placed upon you."

"But . . . if there is no sex at all, Tathagata, would not human life come to an end?"

"Indeed it would, Mahanama, and that is the very outcome we wish for (ASV 11:59; SY 35:28), a perfect empty planet, barren of all life! Another rule regarding Right Action: Avoid singing, dancing and putting on theatrical productions. (ANG 8:41) Moving on, step number five on the Noble Eightfold Path is Right Effort. Right Effort mainly involves crushing, yes, CRUSHING, the sexual desires within yourself. Step Number Six is Right Work."

"What is Right Work, Tathagata?"

"For us, *bikkhus*, it is begging."

"For food, Tathagata?"

"Yes, begging for food. For other people, 'householders,' let us call them, Right Work means refraining from any job that involves weapons. No job involving knives, for instance, is permissible."

"What about knives that are used to slice food, Tathagata?"

"Those knives are fine."

"But couldn't a food-cutting knife also be used as a weapon, Tathagata?"

"Look, knives that are sharp enough to cut food but *not* sharp enough to be weapons, alright?" I paused, looked at the ascetics meaningfully. "Now we reach the two final, yet most important steps of the Noble Eightfold Path, *bikkhus*. Step number seven is *Right Mindfulness*."

"What does it mean, Tathagata?"

"It means to be aware, Assaji. When you are sitting, be aware that you are sitting. When you are walking, be aware that you are walking. When you are defecating, be aware that you are defecating. (DG 22; PP; SP) (By the way, don't defecate standing up; it's a terrible idea for obvious reasons.) (TV) Lastly, step number eight is *Right Concentration*. This means, *bikkhus*, that in order to proceed spiritually, you must learn something very basic—how to *breathe.*"

The monks glanced at each other, unsure. "Do we not breathe all the time, Tathagata?" one said. "Yes, are we not breathing right now?" another added.

"Not in the way *I* am talking about, *bikkhus*. You must not merely 'breathe,' you see, but be *aware* of your breathing." I closed my eyes and demonstrated for them, taking long, deep breaths, then slowly breathing them out. "Breathing in, I think to myself, *'I breathe in, I KNOW I am breathing in.'* Breathing OUT, I think to myself, *'I breathe out, I KNOW I am breathing out.'*" I changed the rhythm of my breathing. "Breathing in short, I think to myself, *'I am breathing in short.'* Breathing out short, I think to myself, *'I am breathing out short.'* My entire body is breathing in and I think to myself, *'My entire body is breathing in.'* Loooong breath in . . . loooong breath out . . ." (SY 54:13)

"It just looks like he's breathing," I heard someone whisper.

I opened my eyes, looked directly at the monks. "You are not where the Buddha is at this point, *bikkhus*. Start where you are, enter the stream, try not to be a degenerate, and in time, and yes, it might be hundreds of billions of years, but in time, you may become an *arahant* like me and go blissfully extinct." (ASV 16:43)

II

The following day, we reconvened.

"You have heard me say again and again that life is nothing but pain, *bikkhus* (ANG 7:70; AP; MV 1:6), but what exactly do I mean by that? I will explain. Starting at the beginning, you spend your first days trapped in your mother's womb—it is fetid and filthy in there. Your excrement floats around you. You try to scream but instead accidentally swallow your own excrement. Consider the loneliness you feel in the womb, *bikkhus,* the bitter and horrible friendlessness. You are alone, trapped in this miserable sewer with no one to help you. This is how your life begins." (ASV 14:32)

I let these words sink in for a moment, then nodded and continued. "Now you are born, *bikkhus.* Imagine the stark terror of it, crushed between two walls. *'Noooooooo,'* you scream, crying out in agony as you enter this brutal world, hot tears streaming down your red, burning cheeks. You don't *want* this. You don't WANT to exist, but you have no choice. The lucky baby, *bikkhus,* is the one who is stillborn, or perhaps severely retarded and thus unable to understand how vile human existence really is." (VK; TGG; DP 11:147–151)

I began to walk among the monks. "Now you grow older, *bikkhus,* you begin to walk and talk, to feed yourself. You begin to forget how horrible life was in the womb, how terrifying it was to be born, how humiliating it was to be a baby and constantly be defecating in your pants. 'Maybe my life will be good,' you begin to think to yourself. 'Maybe everything will turn out alright.' But you are wrong; your life will NOT turn out alright. Now you get sick. You cannot eat, you can barely breathe, perhaps you defecate in your pants again. 'Won't someone please *help me?*' you think to yourself. But no one will help you and do you know why, because no one *can* help you. You begin to waste away, *bikkhus,* to deteriorate. 'I had things I wanted to *do,*' you whimper pathetically, 'but now all I do is suffer.'"

"But perhaps you get better, eh, *bikkhus?* Perhaps you survive your illness, perhaps you thrive and make your way in the world! 'Now I will be truly happy,' you cry determinedly. But you are wrong once again, you will not be 'happy,' you will NEVER be happy, and do you know why not? Because no matter how your life goes, you will *lose things.* (DCP) An example: Let us say that you have a pet monkey whom you love. Let us say that your pet monkey is a charming little rascal, a delightful little scamp who gives you endless happiness. Excellent—but tell me, what do you think will happen when your charming little monkey friend dies, as he inevitably will? You will instantly wish he had never lived—that is what will happen. Another example: Let us say that you have a blanket you love. Do you think the blanket will protect you from suffering? Yes, Vappa?"

"I think it will, if it is cold, Tathagata."

"Ah, but what if it is *hot,* Vappa?"

"Why would you put a blanket over yourself if it was hot, Tathagata?"

"I *wouldn't,* Vappa, why would you?"

"I wouldn't, it would be pointless."

"Precisely and, you see, we are right back where we started! The presence of the blanket will not ease your suffering but the *loss* of the blanket will increase your suffering."

"Are you saying that we should go without blankets then, Tathagata?"

"No, Vappa, without a blanket you will be cold, wishing you had your blanket."

"So ... what are you saying the correct path is then, Tathagata?"

"The correct path, Vappa, is to *have* your blanket but not to *care* about it." (ASV 11:42; ATT 1:2)

As Vappa nodded vaguely, I continued. "But perhaps you will be the lucky one once again, eh, *bikkhu*? Perhaps you will not lose things, perhaps your *karma* will be that good, everything will go well for you, you won't get sick at all, you will live a long, healthy and successful life, congratulations! But guess what, *bikkhus*? You will *still* inevitably get old. Before long your beautiful young body will become withered, bent and unspeakably ugly. 'I cannot see anymore,' you will cry. 'I cannot walk, I cannot control my bowels! I am nothing but a worthless drain on the world, no one loves me, not even my own children (the ones who aren't *dead*, that is, because most of your children will definitely die). All of my friends are dead—I am lonely and terrified and won't someone please *help* me?' But once again, no one will help you because no one *can* help you."

I paused meaningfully, then lowered my voice to something just above a whisper. "And then, *bikkhus*, after all your endless misery, comes the most terrible part of all: *Death*. In the end, after a lifetime of sickness, unhappiness and loss, your final reward will be that your body, which has been a sewer all your life, filled with shit, piss, pus and puke, will now become a *rancid* sewer. (MJ 10; OJO, Humans; SZJ 35; SP; ANG 3:35) That, *bikkhus*, is the true nature of human life."

There was silence for a long moment, before one of the monks, Assaji, asked in a small voice, "Is there not some *joy* in life too, Tathagata?"

"Joy is ephemeral, Assaji. Only pain is permanent"

"But does joy not even *exist*, Tathagata?"

"It does not exist, Assaji, and here is why: Even those things which you think of as 'enjoyable' inevitably cause pain when you lose them. No, *bikkhus,* the one reality, the only reality, is *pain*. Understand that and you can, in time, escape it. Fail to understand that and the following things will inevitably, yes *inevitably,* happen to you: Pain—poverty—broken bones—insanity—legal problems—dead family—burned-down house—Hell. (DP 10) The choice is your, *bikkhus.*"

12

Throughout the early months of my teaching, as my *sangha* was growing, Mara would periodically show up to pester me. "You will *never* escape me, monk," he would jeer at me. "Go away, Mara," I would instantly respond. "I am telling you that you will *never* escape me, monk," he would bluster. "And I am telling *you* to go away, devil!" Mara would stare at me unblinkingly for a few seconds, seemingly surprised by my treatment of him. "The Buddha *knows* me," I sometimes saw in his eyes before he skulked away. Then, not long afterwards, he'd be back. "You are bound by my shackles and you shall **not** escape me, monk!" he would shriek. "Go away, Mara," I would respond, and that would lead to that same exact look: "The Buddha *knows* me," followed by that same exact deflated trudge away. One time I *really* let Mara have it: "You're like a crab with all its legs pulled off," I told him. "You're just a body, unable to move or help itself in any way, honestly. You're a pathetic travesty." (SY 4:1–24; MV 7:15) Lower lip trembling, Mara turned on his heel and speed-walked away.

A number of times Mara showed up while I was meditating, which I found especially irritating. I would feel his presence and glance over and there he would be, twirling his black moustache and smirking at me. He would instantly start yammering, always saying the exact same thing, "You cannot escape me, monk," but I would invariably put him in his place by saying, "You are *nothing*, Mara," at which point he would invariably slink away in defeat. Why he kept coming back, I have no idea; it actually got to be slightly embarrassing at times. "Do you have *no* dignity?" I wanted to ask Mara. One time after I told him to leave, Mara wandered a few feet away and sat on the ground, skinny shoulders slumped, absently poking at the dirt with a stick. (SY 4:24–25) "Why don't you just stop trying, Mara?" I felt like asking him. "You're making a complete fool of yourself."

One night Mara's three daughters, Lust, Appetite and Delight, spoke to him. Their advice, not surprisingly, was terrible. "Don't be sad, father," they told him. "We will catch the Buddha with our snare of lust and bring him under your power!" They flew down and instantly announced to me that they worshipped my feet. I ignored them. They then split themselves into a hundred women, all of whom told me they worshipped my feet. Once again, I ignored them. They then divided themselves into a multitude of women, from young to old, and *all* of them told me they worshipped my feet. "I don't have the 'foot fetish' you all seem to believe I do," I remember thinking to myself at that moment. (SY 4:24–25)

Another strange thing that happened at this time was my fight with a giant snake. I'd had, up to that point, a reasonably good relationship with snakes overall. The day of my great awakening, in fact, as I had approached the Bodhi tree, Kala the Snake-King had kindly informed me that because my splendor "shone forth like the sun," I was on the verge of attaining perfect knowledge. "The birds salute you, soon-to-be Buddha!" Kala the Snake-King had proclaimed (ASV 12:113–15; MV 1:10–15), and that had been very encouraging. For some reason, however, this giant snake now wanted to fight me. It was a brutal fight; before long the hideous creature was blowing fire at me.

Everyone watching the fight was horrified. "That beautiful man is going to be destroyed by that giant, fire-breathing snake!" I heard someone cry. Of course they were mistaken—I was *not* going to be destroyed by the giant fire-breathing snake. Rather, I was going to blow fire right back at him and then stuff him into a huge bowl, which I then gave to the leader of the hermitage I was visiting. Irritatingly, the hermitage's leader didn't seem all *that* surprised by my gift. He also seemed strangely unimpressed when I subsequently parted some waters and flew around. (Among my powers at this time, by the way: Shooting fire out of both my hands and feet; walking through walls; walking on water; turning other people invisible; touching my ears with my tongue.) (DG 11; MV 1:7–54) I finally got sick of this leader's insolence and openly put him in his place. "You're not a Buddha and you're never *going* to be, no matter what you do, understand?" At that point the man dropped to the ground and begged me to teach him. Some people just need a good kick in the ass, you know what I mean? (Shortly after my fight with the giant snake, Mara took the form of a giant snake too. It was a typically moronic move on his part, given that I'd *just* destroyed a giant snake. As usual, I just looked at him and said, "Go away, Mara," and giant-snake-Mara slithered away ignominiously. "That guy is the lamest devil of all time," I remember thinking to myself at that moment.) (SY 4:6)

Before long, my initial group of six followers had grown to sixty, and after that to six hundred. One day in the middle of this growth, two important new students showed up. One of them, Ananda, would turn out to be my closest aide and confidante. The other, Devadatta, would turn out to be my worst enemy. (Sadly, more on Devadatta later.) Ananda was short, balding, heavily built; he blinked a lot, which made him look like he was slightly confused. From the moment Ananda laid eyes on me, it was obvious that all he desired was to serve my every need. For the next forty-plus years, I generously allowed him to do just that. There were moments almost from the start, however, when Ananda was a bit, shall we say, "gushy."

"Master?" I remember him saying to me one night as he washed my feet.

"Hm?"

"I think you are the pure, true mind of the universe."

"Thank you, Ananda."

"I think you are the perfect, empty void of radiance."

"That is very good, Ananda."

"I think you are the one and only reality, master!"

"Again, thank you."

"I think you are an *angel*, master."

"No, Ananda, as I have told you repeatedly, I am merely a man."

"Yes, master, thank you, master."

13

The next day I stood before my growing *sangha*.

"Today I will speak to you regarding the Six Realms of Existence, *bikkhus*. The first realm, the one you find yourself in presently, is of course the human realm. For all the myriad pains involved in human life (and there are *many* of them, obviously, here is a very abbreviated list: leprosy, insanity, being a hunchback or a dwarf, and worst of all by far, being a woman), the human realm is still the best place to be in the universe and I will tell you why: Because it is only those who exist in the human realm who are able to hear the words of the Buddha." (ILL, Humans)

I strolled among the monks. "Below the human realm is the realm of the animals. This is a terrible and frightful place to exist, *bikkhus*, because animals, you see, are pure desire. Animals are so ignorant that they don't even *realize* that their life is suffering. Being eaten alive, for instance, does that sound good to you, *bikkhus*, because *that* is an animal's life. (ASV 14:22–23) Yes, Ananda?"

"Not tigers, master."

" . . . What?"

"Tigers don't get eaten alive."

"No, Ananda, all tigers do is have sex and sleep. Does *that* sound good to you?"

"Uh . . ."

"It shouldn't. Tigers are ignorant fools, Ananda, driven solely by desire."

"Why is one reborn as one animal rather than another, Tathagata?"

"An excellent question, Mahanama. The answer, of course, is *karma*. Here are some specific examples of how *karma* affects reincarnation in the animal realm: If you are a prisoner of your desires in this life, you will be reborn as a goose. If you are a prisoner of your delusions in this life, you will be reborn as a beetle. If you are a prisoner of your conceit in this life, you will be reborn as a donkey. If you are a prisoner of your anger, you will be reborn as a snake-god. (ILL, Animals) What is it *now*, Ananda?"

"What about plants, master?"

"What *about* them?"

"Can one be reborn as a plant?"

"No, Ananda, one cannot be reborn as a plant."

"What about a fungus?"

"No, Ananda, one cannot be reborn as a fungus either."

"Why not, master?"

"I don't *know*, Ananda. I didn't create this system—I'm just describing it to you, now will you *please?* Moving on, the third realm of existence, the one that lies just below that of the animals, is the dreadful realm of the Hungry Ghosts." (LSV 14:29–31; ILL, Ghosts; PV; SH)

"What is a Hungry Ghost, Tathagata?"

"Imagine a creature with an enormous fat belly and a tiny little pinhole mouth, Sariputta."

"How does the Hungry Ghost consume enough to be fat with such a tiny little mouth, Tathagata?"

"The Hungry Ghost is not *fat*, Sariputta, he is *bloated*. His stomach is distended because he is in fact starving. The Hungry Ghost is always *trying* to eat but cannot because his mouth is too small."

"Will the Hungry Ghost eventually die of starvation, Tathagata?"

"It will indeed, Sariputta."

"But . . . a ghost cannot actually die, can it, Tathagata?"

"Everything dies, Assaji, even ghosts."

"Couldn't the Hungry Ghost blend milk and honey together and drink that, Tathagata?"

"No, Vappa, and I will tell you why not: Because if he tried, the milk and honey would instantly change to hot lava, knives or possibly *pus* in his mouth." Reacting to my monks' sickened looks, I nodded: "*Yes, exactly.*"

"Do Hungry Ghosts ever come to the surface of the earth, Tathagata?"

"They do occasionally, Sariputta, in search of food."

"Should we attempt to feed them?"

"You may try, yes, but it will be hopeless because, as I just told you, whatever they eat will turn to either lava, knives or pus in their mouths. Yes, Anuruddha?"

"Do all Hungry Ghosts look the same, Tathagata?"

"An excellent question. No, Anuruddha, they do not. There are some Hungry Ghosts who are, for lack of a better term, more 'ghouls' than 'ghosts.' The dreaded 'Pot Balls,' for instance. Do you know why they are called 'Pot Balls,' Anuruddha?"

"Because . . . their balls are the size of pots, Tathagata?"

"Exactly so, Anuruddha, because their balls are the size of pots, *waterpots*, to be specific. Tell me, do you think walking around with waterpot-balls would be pleasant?"

"No, I think they would smack into each other, Tathagata."

"But mightn't they provide a comfortable cushion to sit on?" I asked.

"I think that sitting on your own balls, especially if they were that swollen, would be enormously painful, Tathagata."

"Well done, Anuruddha, exactly so."

Later that night, as Ananda was massaging my back, he suddenly blurted out: "Ghosts are dead, right, master?"

"Obviously ghosts are dead, Ananda."

"Because I've been thinking about it and I do not understand

. . . How can one be reborn as something that is dead?"

"It's simply the way it is, Ananda. As I told you, I didn't make this system up."

There was silence for a few minutes, then: "Are there *baby* Hungry Ghosts, master?"

"Of course there are baby Hungry Ghosts, Ananda. There are child Hungry Ghosts, adult Hungry Ghosts and eventually, as I also told you, there are dead Hungry Ghosts."

"How is a baby Hungry Ghost *created*, master? Do Hungry Ghosts have sexual intercourse?"

I turned, looked at Ananda. "Hungry Ghosts are reborn from wicked beings who ask too many impertinent questions!"

"I'm so sorry, master."

14

The following day we resumed once again.

"Today we will discuss the next two realms of existence, *bikkhus*, those of the gods and the demigods. First I will speak to you of the realm of the demigods. What exactly *is* a demigod, you may wonder. Answer: Demigods are *like* gods, but not nearly as powerful; they are second rate gods, if you like, and therefore consumed with jealousy for their betters. Yes, Moggallana?"

"Can you give us a specific example of a demigod, Tathagata, because I do not think I comprehend them?"

"Here is one example, Moggallana: The well-known celestial musicians called 'Gandharvas'? (ILL, Ghosts) They are demigods."

"Gandharvas means 'Odor-Eaters,' does it not, Tathagata?"

"Yes, Moggallana, because that is precisely what Gandharvas do, they eat odors. Another demigod would be the half-horse, half-human creature known as the 'Kimnara.'"

"Does the Kimnara have any powers, Tathagata?"

"No, Sariputta, it's just a half-horse, half-human. The truth is, *bikkhus*, that there aren't all that many demigods around when you get down to it and we don't need to spend a lot more time speaking of them. Yes, Mahanama?"

"Would a talking tree count as a demigod, Tathagata?"

"Yes, most certainly."

"What about a half-horse, half-tree?"

"That I am not sure about."

"What about a half-tree, half-*another*-tree?"

"No, Mahanama, that would simply be a tree. Now enough about demigods, as I said they are not particularly important. Let us now move on to the realm of the gods. First, a quick geography lesson, *bikkhus*. The world is flat—we all know that. On top of the earth's flat surface sit the four island continents, each of them situated around Mt. Meru, which is shaped, again as we all know, like a giant cube, with each of its four faces made of a different precious stone. The wall facing our continent, 'Rose Apple Island,' is made of lapis lazuli; that is why when the sunlight hits it the sky turns blue. The gods who live on top of Mt. Meru live for approximately 140,000 years. That sounds like a long time but the gods who live in the skies *above* Mt. Meru live much longer, sometimes for hundreds of millions of years. Far above Mt. Meru lies the Realm of Pure Form. Above *that* is the Formless Realm. The gods who inhabit these realms live for billions of years." (AGG)

"A question for you, *bikkhus*: Do you think these gods are happy? If you think so, you are sadly mistaken, for I tell you they are not. These gods are miserable, more miserable than the worst sinner in Hell and do you know why? Because those suffering in Hell at least know *why* they are being punished; they have been wicked and they know it, while those in heaven have no idea why they suffer. 'But I have been so *good*,' they think. 'Why am I being forced to watch my good *karma* slowly run out? Why are my godly robes becoming filthy and my godly body beginning to stink and my godly eyes beginning to weaken?' Before long, *bikkhus,* these gods are nothing but half-blind, stinking bums, staggering around heaven and waiting to die (because make no mistake, they *do* die, just like everyone else) before being thrown right back into the cesspool of existence. No realm is exempt from the pain of existence, *bikkhus*, not even heaven. That is why I have taught you again and again that the only thing to strive for is *Extinction.*" (OJO, Gods; SDS)

Later that night I was drinking some tea when Ananda dashed in, eyes wide and terrified, trembling like a leaf.

"What is it, Ananda? What's wrong with you?"

"I was meditating under a tree, master—"

"Yes?"

"—when a Hungry Ghost with a flaming mouth showed up before me! He quickly informed me that his name was 'Flaming Mouth' and that I would *die* in three days and afterwards return as a Hungry Ghost exactly like himself! (DFMHG) 'How can I escape this horrible fate, Flaming Mouth?' I pleaded. 'You must feed 100,000 Hungry Ghosts, Ananda,' he told me. 'If you do that, you will *not* become a Hungry Ghost like me after you die. Also, not that you would necessarily have any reason to care about this, but I, Flaming Mouth, will be reborn as a god.'"

"What did you say to Flaming Mouth at that point, Ananda?"

"I said yes, of course I would do it! But master, now I am asking myself, how can I possibly feed 100,000 Hungry Ghosts?"

"You cannot, my friend."

At that, Ananda crumbled to the floor and started sobbing pitifully. "I am *doomed* then, master, oh, *I am dooommmed . . . dooooommmmed . . .*"

I nudged Ananda gently with my foot. "Stop crying, Ananda, you are *not* doomed. There is one way out of this dilemma."

"There *is??*"

"When Flaming Mouth approaches you next, you must speak the following words to him: *'I pay homage to the Tathagata for he is the most revered of all two-legged creatures. I pay homage to the Tathagata of the bejewelled excellence. I pay homage to the Tathagata of the most perfect bodily form and also of vast, unimaginable size. The Tathagata is my Deliverer from Fear and also he is the King of Ambrosia!'"*

"And if I say all that, will Flaming Mouth leave me alone, master?"

"Flaming Mouth will not bother you after that, Ananda, I assure you."

"Oh thank you, master, *thank you thank you thank you*," Ananda whispered as he kissed my feet.

15

"Today we will talk about the most fearsome realm of all, *bikkhus:* Hell. Or perhaps I should say '*Hells,*' because the truth is that there are many of them. (LSV 14:10–14) There are, to begin with, the eight hot Hells and eight cold Hells, all of which lie beneath the surface of the earth, below where the Hungry Ghosts live. In the hot Hells, the flames are so hot that they will literally melt your bones while in the cold Hells, well, let me put it this way—one of the cold Hells is called 'Split like a Blue Lotus.' Do you know why that is, *bikkhus?* Because that is what will happen to the blisters that will form on your naked body there, they will split like blue lotuses! Yes, *exactly.*"

As I strolled among them, I continued: "Moving on to the Secondary Hells. 'Oh,' you may think to yourself, '*Secondary* Hells, that doesn't sound so very frightening.' If you think this, you are deeply mistaken, *bikkhus,* because the truth is that the Secondary Hells are far worse than any of the hot or cold Hells. In Milahakupa Hell, for instance, you will live in a pool of shit and piss while you are endlessly eaten by giant hordes of worms. In Kukkula Hell, you will be cooked and then eaten by birds with metal beaks. After these birds have eaten you, your flesh will then quickly grow back and the birds will eat you again! (ASV 14:14) If you are an adulterer in Kukkula Hell, demons will make you climb a tree of sharp, metal thorns! In Asipattavana

Hell, you will be eaten by dogs with metal fangs! But that's not the worst part of Asipattavana Hell. Guess what your food there will be, *bikkhus*?" (ILL, Hells)

"Feces, Tathagata?"

"Much worse than feces, Anuruddha. Red hot *iron balls*. And what do you think your drink would be?"

"Urine, Tathagata?"

"Again, much worse, Anuruddha. *Molten copper.* But Asipattavana Hell is still not as bad as Vetarani Hell, *bikkhus*. Disagree with the Buddha's ideas in Vetarani Hell and you will end up walking a trail of razor blades where you will be sliced up like a piece of meat before being brought back to life by a sort of 'magic wind,' only to instantly be sliced up again." (OJO, Hells)

"And then brought back to life with more magic wind, Tathagata?"

"No, Moggallana. The second time you die someone will simply *command* you to come back to life. 'LIVE!' they will scream at you and you will live—only to be sliced up like a piece of meat again! Below Vetarani Hell lies Black Rope Hell, *bikkhus*. Here the demons will chop you up with hatchets into 100,000 tiny pieces—yes, they will be very small pieces. After that, the magic wind will blow you back together and the demons will force you to walk a tightrope and when you fall (which you *will*, do not doubt that), it will be directly into a hot cauldron and as you roast in your hot cauldron, do you know what the demons will say to you, *bikkhus*?"

"Burn, fool?"

"That is a decent guess, Sariputta, but no. What the demons will say is, 'You did this to *yourself*, sinner, now *suffer*.' And so you will, for billions of years perhaps. Beneath Black Rope Hell is— yes, Ananda?"

"Does the 'Black Rope' refer to the tightrope, master?"

"Yes, obviously."

"Why is it not called 'Tightrope Hell' then?"

"Because it is called 'Black Rope Hell,' alright, Ananda?

Continuing: Beneath Black Rope Hell is Compounded Hell. Here, once again, you will find trees made of knives, *bikkhus*. But this time there is a cruel twist. This time, at the top of these trees wait nubile young women. When you frantically scramble up a tree to get to one of the women you will be sliced to pieces. Then, when you finally get to the top you will look down and see that same lovely woman on the ground, calling up to you, 'Come to me, my darling, come and *embrace* me.' So you will scurry back down the tree, being cut to pieces once again as you do, but when you get to the bottom of the tree, where do you think the pretty woman will be, eh, *bikkhus*?" (OJO, Hells)

"At the top of the tree, Tathagata?"

"Exactly right. And this up and down will go on for something fairly close to infinity, *bikkhus*."

"Will the men never figure out what's happening to them, Tathagata?"

"No, Assaji, they will not because they are blinded by lust."

"You'd think they'd figure it out *eventually*."

"Well, they will not."

"What about the women in the trees, master?"

"What about them, Moggallana?"

"How are *they* being punished?"

"They are *women,* Moggallana. That is punishment in itself."

That night at bedtime, as we laid in the darkness: "Master?"

"What is it, Ananda?"

"Is it bad that I don't *hate* the idea of the cold Hells?" I half-turned, looked at him. "What I mean is, being frozen doesn't sound *that* terrible to me. Being a block of ice and then maybe being reborn as a talking tree or a two-headed horse—"

"First of all, Ananda, I never said anything about two-headed horses. Secondly, you wouldn't be a 'block of ice' in a cold Hell. You would be in frozen *agony*, covered with open blisters, naked and shrieking in pain for billions of years before you were reborn, not as a demigod perhaps, but as a Hungry Ghost or even a demon."

"Yes, master. Thank you, master."

"Now go to sleep."

"You are so very good to me, master."

‍फ़

Sometimes during these *sangha*-building years I would venture into a village to speak to the people who lived there, the "householders," as I called them. These conversations, I will not lie, were at times frustrating. I had known from the beginning obviously that there would be many people who would have far too much "dust in their eyes" to grasp my profound ideas. I had expressed that very misgiving to Brahma, in fact, so many years before. It was never easy dealing with such debased souls. I remember one particular householder, a man in his late forties, stocky and broad-faced, looking at me one day and saying, "But there are people who *enjoy* children, sir."

"They may *think* they enjoy children, but they are mistaken. What they are experiencing is not 'joy,' you see, but rather misery. I repeat, do not love your children, my friends, rather *detach* from them; detach from *everyone* beloved to you, in fact." (RH)

"But what exactly is wrong with *love*, sir?" the stocky man continued.

"Love is nothing but a trap, my friend. (MJ 39: SZJ 21) Consider the following situation, if you will: You have a beloved. 'How I hope my beloved doesn't die,' you think to yourself. Then, not long afterwards, 'Oh, now my beloved is dead and I am so terribly sad.' Cut off all your feelings for this person, however, and you will not fear their death, nor will you grieve it. For the man set free of love in this manner (and I am speaking now of love for a specific person obviously because it goes without saying that you should love all living beings in the entire universe just like I do), for this liberated man, there is no pain. 'Let my beloved get sick and die, I feel nothing,' is what he will think."

"Are you saying that it is *wrong* to care for others, sir?"

"I am saying that it is *right* to care for *yourself* and to let others do the same." (SY 47:9–13)

"I have a child, sir, a son," interjected a second, taller householder. "It is very important to me that he be well and happy. I cannot understand what is wrong with that feeling."

"Let me ask you this, friend," I replied. "If your son was killed tomorrow, would you be sad about it?"

"I would be utterly bereft, sir."

"And this is because you are *attached* to your son, correct?"

"Yes, of course."

"But tell me, my friend, before your son was born were you attached to him?"

"Was I—? Well, no, because he didn't *exist* yet."

"So it was only once he *existed* that you became attached to him, is that right?"

"Ye-es."

"But if he was killed then he would not exist anymore, would he?" (SY 42:11)

"What? I don't . . ."

"My son Rahula could be slowly and horribly tortured to death and I would not even care. *This* is what you should aspire to, friends."

The stockier householder piped up once again. "I for one quite *like* life, sir."

"I'm sure you *think* you do."

"No, sir, I *do* like life. I like sunshine, for instance."

"Ah, but what about rain?"

"I like rain too. I like the cool water."

"Ah, but what about scalding hot water?"

The taller householder spoke up. "You are the most negative person I've ever met, sir."

I smiled, bemused. "I tell you that life is pain and love is a trap and that the only worthy goal is death, and you find these ideas *negative?*"

"I think life is wonderful," the taller householder suddenly announced, and now he and the stockier man started going back and forth. "I love my wife, for instance . . ." "Yes, and our children and our little house . . ." "I love to eat . . ." "And to sleep and to bathe . . ."

"*Shut up, you defiled imbeciles,*" I thought to myself.

"I love to laugh," the stocky man proclaimed. "I even love to *cry* sometimes," the taller man added. Another man, small and wiry, joined in. "I like singing and dancing!" Then a fourth man: "I like being with my friends."

"*You are all delusional morons, all of you.*"

The householders looked at me. "We all love being *alive*, sir. For whatever time we get." "Yes, we don't want life to end, why would we want *that?*" "Because what if this life is all there is? Why would we want to shut it down?"

"What I am telling you, my friends, is that the one thing that truly matters is *pain*."

"But what makes you think that is true for *everyone,* sir, what makes you think it's not just true for *you?*"

I stared at the householders for a moment, unsure how to even respond to such a ludicrous question. "Wicked men abusing good men are spitting up at heaven," I finally said. "They'd better be prepared to be drenched in spit." (SOA; SZJ 7)

The tall man looked at me, clearly surprised. "Are you saying that we are wicked men and you are a good man, sir?"

"I am not saying that I am a 'good man,' no, I am saying that I am a 'perfect man.'"

"Is that really for *you* to say, sir?"

I rose to my full height and faced them all down. "I am worth sixteen times what any of you is worth." And with that, I turned and walked away. (DP 5:70)

Later that night, as he finished massaging my scalp, Ananda looked at me nervously. "Master?"

"Yes, Ananda?"

"Do you remember when you asked me to more fully articulate your perfection?" (DG 14; ACC 3:118–24)

"I do."

"I have written a story attempting to do so. May I read it to you?"

"That sounds lovely, old friend, go ahead."

Ananda smiled, stood up. He closed his eyes and started reciting his story, speaking in a stiff, overly formal way and punctuating his words with self-conscious arm movements. "*Hear me now! The Buddha is like a thousand suns, each one more perfect than the last! The Buddha's eyes are large and pure, like two beautiful pools of flower-filled water! The Buddha's teeth are white like rice and also they are perfectly even, very nice and close together with no unsightly gaps at all!*"

"That's charming, Ananda, thank you."

"*The Buddha is like the ocean! Infinite jewels reside within him, fish and clams and lobsters and starfish and many other aquatic creatures reside within him!*"

"Wonderful, thank y—."

"*The Buddha's webbed hands are elegant, as are his webbed feet! The Buddha is like a king, to be specific, a Goose King!*"

"Thank you, Ana—"

"*The Buddha is like a mountain, grand, lofty and monumental! Bow your head to the magnificence of Buddha Mountain!*"

"Ananda, stop . . ."

"*You could not possibly understand the Buddha's greatness because it is far too vast for you to comprehend! Bow down to Buddha Mountain, I say again, bow down to this holy mountain of a thousand perfect suns!*"

"Is that . . . it?"

"Do you like it, master?"

"I do, Ananda, thank you. But now we need to rest, my friend."

"Did you like how I filled your bath with lotus flowers earlier this evening, master?"

"I did, Ananda, yes."

"Did you like how I covered your bed with lotus flowers too?"

"Yes."

"Did you notice that I rubbed lotus flowers into your robe, to scent it with their delightful fragrance?"

"Yes, that was fine."

"I could think of no other place to put lotus flowers, master, but now I am wondering, would you like me to rub some in your hair?"

"No, Ananda, and that's enough, now stop talking."

"Yes, master, I'm sorry. I love you, master."

17

At this point in the story something unfortunate happened: Women took center stage for a while.

The first thing I had to deal with was several of my students struggling to resist, shall we say, "feminine charms." (ATT 7:9) "I have heard, *bikkhus,* that some of you have been struggling with lustful thoughts," I told them. "I wish to help you with this. In order to do so, I need you to please close your eyes. Good. Now please imagine a sixteen-year-old girl. Imagine that this girl has exquisite form and shape, that she is lovely in every conceivable way. Do you have this girl in mind, *bikkhus*? Excellent. Now please think of this exact same girl at ninety years of age. Ah, not so attractive now, is she? Crooked, isn't she? Hunched and toothless, with milky eyes and thin grey hair, withered and blotchy, frankly a hag, isn't she? Do you have this hag in mind, *bikkhus*? Good. Now please imagine her as not only old but also sick. Imagine her laying in a pool of her own urine and excrement and please tell me: Do you desire her *now*? If so, please imagine this sickly crone a few years later still. She's dead now, *bikkhus*, a corpse dumped on the ground, three days dead, bloated and oozing fluid, picked at by both dogs and birds. Do you still desire her? How about a few days later when she's nothing but a bloody skeleton? Or a few weeks after that when she's a pile of bones? Or after that when she's nothing but a pile of *dust?* What do you think of your lovely sixteen-year-old girl *now*, eh, *bikkhus?*" (SP; MHD 1:84–90)

As I walked among my monks, I continued: "The desire for sexual pleasure is like the desire which lepers, covered with sores and eaten by worms, feel to scratch their foul-smelling wounds, *bikkhus.* The more the lepers scratch, the more infected the wounds get, yet they continue to scratch anyway and why? Because they are unable to *stop* themselves. Listen to me now, *bikkhus,* and listen well: There is no disaster in the world worse than sexual pleasure, none." (DP 14; MGD 1:504–08)

From the back of the group came a small voice: "Have you yourself ever had to overcome lust, Tathagata?"

"Of course I have, *bikkhu,* I understand lust extremely well. To illustrate, let me tell you a story about one of my previous lifetimes. I was a golden peacock, so beautiful that I was frankly disconcerting to others. One day I remember drinking from a pool, looking down and seeing my own reflection in the water and thinking to myself, 'It's true, I really *am* the most stunning peacock in the world. My beauty could literally be dangerous to others. I should hide myself away.' Which I did, *bikkhus*—but sadly I was spotted by some greedy humans who quickly became obsessed with the idea of catching me. But they always failed to do so and do you know why, *bikkhus?*"

"Because you outsmarted them, Tathagata?"

"I *did* outsmart them, Moggallana, that is definitely true, but they also failed to catch me because I was *holy* and my holiness protected me. (I was also extremely charming, I forgot to mention that, but I was.) But—and this is the relevant part of the story for you, *bikkhus*—I had one weakness: *Females.* A human hunter took advantage of this weakness by tempting me with a peahen (the hunter actually taught the peahen to *dance,* which was undeniably impressive, just not something you see very often), but when I approached her, he quickly captured me. That's right, *bikkhus,* the Buddha was captured."

"What happened then, Tathagata?"

"I had a long talk with the hunter, Sariputta. We discussed right and wrong, morality in general, and before long he understood that killing me would be wrong. He renounced being a hunter, but that was not good enough for me; I told him that he needed to perform an Act of Truth (that's how I put it, an Act of Truth) by freeing ALL birds, which he did. All birds have been free from that day forward, all *animals* have been free in fact—there has never been one single captive animal since then, thanks to me, *bikkhus.* Then in the end the hunter and I flew away together." (GPJAT)

"The hunter could *fly,* Tathagata?"

"Oh yes."

There was a long moment of silence before: "I'm sorry, Tathagata, but I don't quite understand what *harm* lust did to you in that story?"

"I was *captured,* Mahanama. As great and holy and beautiful and charming as I was, I was captured and nearly *killed* and all because of an attractive dancing peahen. Now granted, in this *particular* story, it all turned out for the best but still, the point is that lust is very bad, *bikkhus.*"

Now another voice from near the back of the group: "But women can be so *attractive, Tathagata.*"

"Indeed they can, *bikkhu,* very attractive and very tempting. Here is the story of another previous lifetime, relating to that very point. This story is called 'Goblin Town.' Once I was a flying horse with a bird's head. I was named 'Cloud Horse.'" (GTJAT; PP 1)

"Did you say you were a flying horse with a *bird's head,* Tathagata?"

"That's exactly what I said, Anuruddha. As Cloud Horse, I lived near an island which was populated entirely by women. These women lured shipwrecked men to the island by telling them that they wanted the men to be their husbands. What these women wanted, in fact, was to *eat* the men. But do you know who saved the men from these she-demons?"

"You, Tathagata?"

"Correct, Anuruddha, me. I flew over the island and called down to the men, 'Who wants to be saved?' The ones who answered yes, I took home. The others, well, I left them to be eaten by the women. So tell me—what is the *moral* of this story, *bikkhus*?"

After a brief pause and some sidelong glances: "That Cloud Horse will save you, Tathagata?"

"No, Vappa, that is far too literal. The moral of the story is this: 'Those who ignore the Buddha's words will perish, while those who listen to the Buddha's words will be saved.'" There was silence for a moment as I let this sink in. Then I lowered my voice. "I will not mince words with you, *bikkhus*: It would be better for your penis to go into the mouth of a poisonous snake or a pit of hot coals than into a woman, and do you know why? Because while the first two would definitely cause you to lose your penis, the third would cause you to lose your *soul*. This is what you must understand about women, monks: They want to give birth, giving birth is part of their defiled nature. But when they do give birth, what, I ask you, are they giving birth to? *To pain and nothing else.* Women are not your friends, *bikkhus*. Loathe them. They are sacks of filth ... ogres ... demons ... hags." (SZJ 24; IOU)

That night, as we were sipping our tea: "Master?"

"Hm?"

"Why was that story called 'Goblin Town'?"

"What?"

"Wouldn't 'Demon Island' have made more sense? Or 'The Story of Cloud Horse'? Was there even a goblin in the story?"

"You have, as always, completely missed the point, Ananda."

"I'm so sorry, master."

"Yes, well—apology not accepted."

18

Not long after that, another female problem arose: My stepmother Prajapati showed up, wanting to join my *sangha*. "My son," she murmured quietly as she entered my chamber and bowed down before me. (CV 10:1)

"*Stepson*," I quickly responded

"... What's that?" she said, looking up at me with her weathered old face.

"Stepson. While I recognize that you were *like* a mother to me, you were not *actually* my mother. I am your stepson and you should call me that."

"Do you know why I am here, Siddhartha?"

"I do and I am sorry, Aunt, but what you ask is simply not possible."

"Why?"

"Women inspire lust in men, Aunt, and I will not allow lust to enter the *sangha*."

"I am *old*, Siddhartha."

"You are old, Aunt, that is certainly true. But not all women are old. Some are young and attractive and those women, I assure you, would quickly become dangerous to the *sangha*."

"I beg of you, my son, as the woman who *raised* you—"

"Again, Aunt, please, *stepson*. Understand this is not in any way personal, it is simply that women are, how best to put this, defiled."

"Women are *human beings*, Siddhartha, just like you."

I quickly stood up. "I am sorry, Aunt, but I cannot honor your request. Good luck on your journey home." With that, I turned and walked away from her. (ANG 8:51)

At first I thought I had handled my "woman problem" but the truth was that it was about to get *much* worse. Because not long afterwards Yasodhara sat before me. I stared at her in chilly silence for a long moment before she finally spoke.

"I have missed you, husband. We have both missed you, Rahula and I."

"Ah yes. How is Rahula?"

"He is well, husband. He looks just like you."

I nodded vaguely. A moment passed, then: "To get to the point here, Yasodhara, I understand that, like my aunt, you wish to join my *sangha*, is that correct?"

"Yes, husband."

I studied her for a moment, stroked my chin. "How old are you now, Yasodhara?"

"Thirty-eight, husband."

"You look quite well. Prajapati is old and ugly (her words, by the way, not mine), but you, Yasodhara, you would surely be a distraction within the *sangha*, whether you wished to be or not."

"I would do anything to be near you, husband."

"I'm sorry, Yasodhara, but the answer must be no. Good luck on your journey home."

As I stood and started to exit the room, Yasodhara grabbed my arm. "You speak so much of compassion, husband, but will you show no compassion for *me*? Will you show no compassion for poor Rahula?" (MSV; ASV 9:28–34)

"Stop it, Yasodhara."

"He searched for you endlessly, Siddhartha, haunting the palace every night and whimpering to himself, 'Papa, where are you? *Papa, please, where are you??*'"

"The pain you are describing was caused merely by ignorance, Yasodhara."

"How can you be so *brutal*, husband?"

"Calm yourself, Yasodhara."

"You have *hurt me*, Siddhartha."

"Life has hurt you, Yasodhara. Life hurts us all."

*"No, husband, you— YOU—**you** have hurt me."* I turned and started out of the room, but Yasodhara rose and followed me. "I was like a widow, Siddhartha, I cried for months, for *years*." (LSV 8:31–9:35; BL)

"You need to *calm down*, Yasodhara. And please stop calling me Siddhartha. I am the Buddha now."

"I *loved* you, Siddhartha, god help me. I love you still. Oh please allow me to be near you, husband, please my darling, *please* . . ."

"Yasodhara—"

"I am your lawful wife, Siddhartha. I am your lawful . . ." With that, she began to sob, moaning through her tears, "I . . . am . . . so . . . wretched."

I hesitated for a long moment, then sat down next Yasodhara and spoke to her in a soft, calming voice. "I would like to tell you a story now, Yasodhara."

As she looked up at me through her tears: "It is no surprise that you love me the way you do, Yasodhara. The truth is that you have *always* loved me this way, in every single lifetime we have shared. That's right, Yasodhara, you and I have known each other many times before. In one particular lifetime, for instance, I was a fairy named Canda who lived in the mountains and you were my fairy wife, also named Canda." (FCJAT)

" . . . I was named Canda too?"

"Yes, we were both fairies named Canda who ate pollen and dressed in flowers and danced around, isn't that charming? One day, however, a wicked human shot me with an arrow (the human was apparently attracted to *you,* Yasodhara, because you were quite a pretty little fairy, yes you were) and my life was in grave danger until you talked Brahma into helping me and so I lived, isn't that marvelous, Yasodhara, I lived because of *you.* You were devoted to me, you see, as you always have been and as you always will be. I hope that makes you feel better."

She grabbed my hand and kissed it, pressing it to her tear-stained face. "Let me learn from you . . . Buddha?"

That night as we were eating dinner, Ananda glanced over at me. "Could you not find *some* way of allowing Prajapati and Yasodhara to be part of the *sangha,* master?"

"No, Ananda, I could not and please stop asking me about it."

"I do so only because Prajapati and Yasodhara are not going away, master. They are continuing to follow us everywhere we go."

"I am fully aware of that, Ananda."

"We have told them to leave but they won't listen. Their feet are bleeding very badly, master."

"Yes, and that is because they are not *made* for this life, Ananda. They do not belong here, which is my point exactly."

Ananda and I ate in silence for a long moment. Then: "Can women not even *achieve* enlightenment, master?"

"Hmm?"

"Can women not even achieve enlightenment? Is enlightenment only for men?"

"Women *can* achieve enlightenment, of course, Ananda, *theoretically* speaking. But what Prajapati and Yasodhara are asking of me simply cannot occur and fine, I will tell you why. I have never disclosed the following to you or anyone else, Ananda, so brace yourself: My perfect wisdom will only last for one thousand years." (CV 10:1)

"Oh master, no!"

"I'm afraid so."

"But *why?*"

"That I don't know, it's simply the way things are. My insights will resonate for a thousand years and after that be completely forgotten."

"That is awful, master!"

"But that is not all, Ananda. If women were to enter the *sangha,* my words would not last a thousand years but rather, prepare yourself, *five hundred* years." (ANG 8:51)

"Oh no!"

"For just as when mold strikes, the crops are doomed, if women were to strike the *sangha,* it too would be doomed."

An hour later, at bedtime, out of the blue: "What if women were *inferior* to men, master?"

"What do you mean by *inferior,* Ananda?"

"I don't know exactly, just . . . inferior in every way. Mightn't that work?"

I started to speak, then stopped and considered Ananda's question.

৭

"I have decided that women may join the *sangha*, Ananda," I announced over tea the next morning. (CV 10:1)

"Oh, master!"

"But only under the following condition: That they play an *inferior* role in the community."

"Yes, master, of course!"

"One example: A woman who has been a nun for, let us say, fifty years meets a man who has been a monk for, let us say, *one day*. The woman is still the man's inferior, she must defer to him, she must pay her respects to him. This one-day monk may criticize this fifty-year nun all he wishes for as long as he wishes but she may not criticize him at ALL, *EVER*." (TV)

"Prajapati will be so happy, master, oh, this is such exciting news."

"No, Ananda, it is not exciting news. It is, in fact, terrible news. Allowing women into the *sangha*, as I already told you, will cut in half the period of time during which my profound teachings will illuminate the world."

"Oh . . . Oh yes, master . . ."

"Please stop smiling like that, Ananda."

A few days later, I stood before a small group of women, my *sangha*'s first nuns. At the front of the group was Prajapati; behind her was Yasodhara; behind her were many others. "Have you any lessons for us, Tathagata?" Prajapati asked me.

"I do, nuns. Please imagine a butcher, if you will. Please imagine that this butcher is killing a cow and carving it up with an extremely sharp knife. Imagine that the butcher cuts away all the cow's flesh and organs, leaving only the cow's hide. Have you imagined all this? Good. Now a question for you, nuns: If the butcher were to hold up the cow's hide and pronounce, '*This is the cow,*' would he be lying or speaking the truth? It still *looks* like the cow, but as it has been gutted and there is literally nothing left inside it, tell me, *is* it in fact the cow?" (NKV 3:274–75)

Some of the women glanced at each other, unsure. Finally Prajapati spoke. "We do not know, Tathagata."

"Then I will tell you: The butcher is telling the truth, the empty hide *is* the cow. In fact, it is a superior *version* of the cow because the flesh and organs that the butcher cut away represented lust and desire. The butcher's sharp knife represented noble wisdom removing these impurities and, when you get right down to it, the butcher basically represented me."

The women stared at me in evident confusion for a moment. "Are you saying that the hollowed out version of the cow is *better*, Tathagata?"

"Indeed I am, nun, for it is better for the cow, far better, to be an empty husk than to experience desire."

The women were silent for a moment, then one of them asked, "Have you yourself ever been a woman, Tathagata?"

"I have indeed, sister, and thank you for asking. Once, nuns, in a previous lifetime, I was a beautiful, intelligent and charming queen named Rubyavarti. Sadly, there was a famine in my country. People were slowly starving to death, some of them were literally preparing to eat their own children. I knew I had to do something to help people and so, as a woman, I did the one thing that no man could possibly do: I fed others with my body."

"You breast-fed your people, Tathagata?"

"In a manner of speaking. I cut my breasts off and people ate them." (RUJAT)

" . . . You cut your breasts off?"

"People were extremely impressed with my decision to do so. 'Rubyavarti's wise choice contrasts with her sex!' they cried in joy. Afterwards, of course, my husband wished for my beautiful breasts to grow back and they magically did, but then do you know what happened, nuns?"

"You cut your breasts off again to feed more people, Tathagata?"

"That is an excellent guess, nun, but no. What actually happened is that the king of the gods came to me and asked what I wished for most of all and I told him, 'My one and only wish is to be a man.' He then granted my wish and I became a man. So you see, nuns, by cutting off my breasts I escaped the horrible fate of being a woman. Isn't that an excellent story?"

The women stared at me in silence.

As we were heading back to our chambers, Ananda turned to me: "Master?"

"What is it, Ananda?"

"Why would a butcher *do* such a thing?"

" . . . What?"

"Why would a butcher cut all the meat off a cow and then stitch it back together as an empty husk?"

"Oh be quiet, Ananda."

"Yes, master, I'm so sorry, master."

I did have one moderately successful encounter with a woman during this stretch of time. It occurred when I flew up to heaven and visited my dead mother there. (MV 10:1)

"Siddhartha?" Mother whispered in amazement when she first saw me. She rushed to embrace me but I pushed her away. "I am not here to hug you, Mother. I am here to teach you the truth regarding Absolute Reality."

"But my son—"

"We will begin with the Four Noble Truths, Mother."

"But Siddhartha—"

"Do you want to hear about my profound insights or not?"

"Yes . . . yes, of course I do, my son," she whispered. I lectured my mother for the next hundred hours. She mainly sat silently and listened to me, but at one point she did interject. "But my son," she murmured, "life is not *all* pain, is it? Here you are before me, for instance, my beloved Siddhartha, and there is no pain in *that*." Once again, she tried to embrace me; once again, I rebuffed her. "Soon I will leave you again, Mother, and you will never see me again because soon I will be extinct, so think of the pain of *that*, eh?" I replied. That shut her up.

After I finished describing Absolute Truth to my mother, I rose and started to leave. She touched my arm. "Please, Siddhartha, before you go, tell me, did you *marry*? Did you become a father? Am I a grandmother, my son?"

I hesitated, sighed. "I married and had a son, Mother."

"What is his name?"

"Rahula."

"Rahu—? But Siddhartha, that means '*shackle*.'"

"Exactly, because that's what Rahula was to me, Mother, a shackle, as was my wife, Yasodhara. I left them both the day Rahula was born because that was when I first understood that attachments were nothing but traps and that I was not going to be trapped and *please stop crying Mother or I will leave immediately*."

When she didn't stop crying I left and as I flew back down to earth, I remember thinking to myself, "Why did I even *bother* with that?"

20

Yasodhara's return to my life brought a second problem with it: Rahula. He was eleven years old now, quite handsome like me, but somewhat sour-looking, I thought. He was around a great deal and I often had no idea what to say to him. One night as he was washing my feet, however, I had an idea. "Do you see the water in your dipper, Rahula?" (MJ 61)

"Yes, Father."

"Unless you are careful to avoid lies, you will be no better than that dipper," I said, then roughly knocked the water out of the dipper onto the floor. "Did you see what I just did, Rahula?"

"Yes, Father."

"Unless you are careful to avoid lies, whatever is good in you will be lost in that same exact way." Now I grabbed the dipper out of his hand and turned it upside down. "Do you see what I am doing *now*, Rahula?"

"Yes, Father."

"Unless you are careful to avoid lies, you will become nothing but an empty vessel, like this dipper." As Rahula stared back at me, I could see confusion in his eyes; "But Father, I'm not lying," he was clearly thinking. Which was true, he *wasn't* lying, he wasn't even *saying* anything, how could he have been lying? A moment later, I tried a different approach. "Imagine an elephant, eh, Rahula? Imagine that this elephant is large, powerful and battle-hardened. Until this elephant has devoted his life to the king, however, Rahula, I tell you that he is not fully trained. Similarly, unless you avoid telling lies, *you* are not fully trained." (RAH)

Again, Rahula stared back at me in obvious confusion. I found myself shifting uncomfortably. "The point I am trying to make here is that I am like a lion, Rahula, the king of all beasts. People are *scared* of me is what I am getting at, they tremble before me. 'But we thought we were *permanent*, Tathagata,' they whine to me. 'Well, guess what, fools, you're *not* permanent, you're impermanent, just like everything else.' That makes them shit, just like elephants do in my presence. Do you see my point?" (SY 22:78)

Still Rahula was silent. I turned away and shook my head. "This is why I left when he was a baby," I remember thinking to myself. "To avoid moments exactly like *this*."

A few years later, Rahula was sitting under a tree and meditating. "Try to be like the earth, Rahula," I instructed him. "When people drop disagreeable things on the earth, shit for instance, the earth is not upset; the earth doesn't even *care*. Or better yet, try to be like space, Rahula. *Nothing* bothers space and do you know why? Because 'space' is *nothing*. Be like that, be nothing."

Rahula opened his eyes and stared directly at me. I instantly felt myself stiffen. "You must get rid of your ill will," I informed him. "You are filled with cruelty and resentment. I can see it in your eyes." (MJ 62)

Still he stared at me. I turned and walked away.

That night after dinner I sat Rahula down. "As you presumably know, Rahula, I have perfect remembrance of all my previous lifetimes."

"Yes, Father."

"I would like to tell you about the lifetime that occurred *just prior* to this one and was, consequently, extremely important. I was Prince Vessantara, Rahula, a great being, not necessarily 'perfect' yet but definitely 'great.' (VSJAT) One of the things that made me so great was my extraordinary generosity. To give you an idea, when I was born (which I had to do through my mother's birth canal, which was utterly disgusting, but never mind that right now), I emerged talking. 'Is there anything I can give away, Mother?' I instantly asked. 'I wish to give to charity!' When my mother agreed, I roared like a little lion, Rahula, that's how happy I was to be so generous." (NK)

Rahula nodded, looking vaguely unsure.

"My wife in this previous lifetime was named Maddi, Rahula, and one night she had a terrible nightmare. She came rushing into my chambers in the middle of the night, begging me to comfort her. 'Why are you here?' I demanded of her. 'I have had a nightmare, Prince Vessantara.' But when Maddi described her nightmare to me, Rahula, I was not in the least disturbed by it. Rather I was *elated* by what I heard. Because I instantly understood that Maddi's dream was *prophetic* and what it prophesied was that I was just about to fulfill the Perfection of Giving! Do you know how I was going to do that, Rahula?"

"No, Father."

"I was going to give my children away!"

" . . . What?"

"'You ate some bad meat, woman,' I told Maddi. 'Go back to your bed, there's nothing to your nightmare.' I knew this wasn't true, of course. I *knew* Maddi's nightmare was prophetic but I told her otherwise out of compassion for her. The following day Maddi left our two children in my care. 'Protect them, my Lord,' she implored me as she went off in search of food. (Why a princess had to go off in search of food I'm still not entirely sure of, but no matter, moving on.) Not long after Maddi left, a man came to the house, Rahula. He was fat, filthy and deformed, with rotten teeth. He was horrible-looking really, he barely even looked human. But when this monstrous creature asked for my children, do you know what I felt at that moment, Rahula?"

"Pain?"

"Oh no no, on the contrary, I was filled with *happiness*, Rahula!"

"Please do not say that, Father."

"'Why of course you may have my children,' I quickly cried to the vile man. 'Their mother is gone and they are all yours!' 'You should know that I intend to use them as slaves,' the hideous man told me."

"*Father, no . . .*"

"'Splendid, you are their master!' I instantly replied. The children did not want to go with the horrid man obviously, Rahula, so I leaned down and got very close to my son's face and whispered to him, 'Fulfill Daddy's perfection now, son. Consecrate daddy's heart. Do you not know that *giving* brings Daddy happiness, son? Do you not want Daddy to be happy?'"

"But he was your *son* . . ."

"'Omniscience,' I suddenly proclaimed in a loud voice, 'is a hundred—no, a thousand—no, a *hundred thousand times more precious to me than the lives of my own children!*'"

"Father, please . . ."

"Do you know what my son said to me as he was led away, Rahula? He looked back at me and said, 'May you be happy, Daddy.' Isn't that adorable? 'May you be be happy,' so darling. Now I *will* admit that as I watched that loathsome man drive my children away, I was torn, Rahula."

"You were?"

"Oh yes. For a moment I even considered running after them, killing the man and bringing my children back."

"You did?"

"On second thought, however, I decided not to. To take back a gift simply because of the suffering of young children—well, that is simply *not* what a good man would do, Rahula. It was painful to see my children beaten by this appalling creature, do not misunderstand me. But once a gift has been given you *don't* take it back, that is the larger point. As the man led my children away, beating them, my girl turned back and cried out, 'How can you just watch this happen, Daddy?' Which was, honestly, amusing in a way, because she did not realize that by watching my children taken away I had just overcome a great flaw: The flaw of *affection*, Rahula."

Rahula began to weep. After a moment, I patted his head lightly. "You may continue in the *sangha*, Rahula. Not as my 'son' obviously, for I feel no attachment to you in that way, none whatsoever, but as a monk."

"Thank you, Father," Rahula murmured, then off my look, corrected himself: "Thank you, *Buddha*." I offered my hand and he kissed it.

At the age of twenty, Rahula finally became a full-fledged member of the *sangha*. I remember the day well. Rahula sat in front of the whole community as I slowly walked around him, peppering him with questions. "Tell me, monk," I demanded in a stern voice, "is the eye permanent or impermanent?" (MV 1:6; SY 22:45–78; MJ 147)

"Impermanent, Tathagata!"

"And is the impermanent pleasant or unpleasant, monk?"

Rahula and I had worked on this particular question a great deal. When we had first begun (and for some time thereafter, to be honest), he had occasionally responded with, "Could not impermanence be *pleasant,* Tathagata?"

"No, Rahula. Change is painful in every case."

"But what if things change for the *better*?" he would sometimes persist.

"That is not possible."

"Would not the cessation of pain be positive change, Tathagata?"

"Truly understood, Rahula, pain never ceases." (DP 11:147)

In front of the *sangha*, Rahula hesitated for a long moment, then called out in a strong voice, "All change is unpleasant, Tathagata!"

"And what is the goal of life, monk?" I demanded.

"Extinction, Tathagata!"

"Excellent, monk. Well done."

21

As I mentioned earlier, at the same time that Ananda had entered my *sangha*, a second man, Devadatta, had joined too. Devadatta was Yasodhara's brother, as well as my distant cousin. He was tall and lean with coal black eyes and a blank, even indifferent expression on his face.

I remember the first time Devadatta openly challenged me. I was telling the noble story of my interactions with a young woman named Kisa Gotami. "Kisa Gotami gave birth to a beautiful child, *bikkhus*," I had told my monks, "whom she loved very dearly. One day, however, the child died quite suddenly and Kisa Gotami was distraught with grief. No one could comfort her, she carried her dead child around with her for days on end. Fortunately, *bikkhus*, I myself was passing her village at the time and, knowing of my reputation, Kisa Gotami ran up to me and begged for my help. 'Please bring my dead child back to life, Tathagata?' she pleaded. I informed Kisa Gotami that I could indeed bring her child back to life, but only under one condition: That she gather mustard seeds from every home in the village that had *not* experienced death. Tell me, *bikkhus*: What do you think happened at that point?" (MUS; THR)

"Every house Kisa Gotami went to *had* experienced death, Tathagata?"

"Correct, Sariputta. Very good. Yes, Devadatta?"

"I am wondering, Tathagata—what would have happened if Kisa Gotami *had* in fact found a house that hadn't experienced death?"

"She wasn't *going* to, Devadatta. I obviously knew that."

"But with all due respect, Perfect One, not *all* houses have experienced death. There are newer houses, for instance, filled with younger families. What if Kisa Gotami had gone to one of those?"

I stared coldly at Devadatta. "You are missing the point of my story, Devadatta. The point is that once Kisa Gotami understood that all, yes ALL, houses experience death, she became enlightened."

"I understand that, Perfect One, I am simply asking: Would you *actually* have been capable of bringing Kisa Gotami's child back from the dead if for some strange reason she *had* found a house that hadn't experienced death?"

I decided to turn things back on Devadatta. "A question for *you*, *bikkhu*: Suppose that you were wounded by an arrow smeared with poison and that your friends brought in a doctor to help you. Would you say to your friends, 'I will not allow this doctor to help me until I know the name of the man who shot the arrow at me, whether he was tall or short, dark- or light-skinned, whether he used a long bow or a crossbow, what kind of feathers he used on his shaft, what kind of arrowhead he used?' If you said these things, you would soon be *dead*, Devadatta. So too with your pointless questions." (CV 1:426–32)

"I see."

"No, Devadatta, I don't think you do see. Honestly, trying to explain things to you can be like trying to describe the color of the sky to a blind man. The blind man can't possibly understand the color of the sky. What he *can* understand is that he is blind and that his blindness is why he suffers. I am trying to help that blind man understand this but he will not stop asking me what color the sky is and it's *blue*, alright, but does that mean anything to the blind man, *no!* Please understand, Devadatta, that there are *many* things I know that I do not teach you. What I teach you is like this one leaf; what I actually know is like all the leaves on all the trees in this grove." (SY 56:21)

"And you say this not out of 'ego,' obviously, because, as you have so often told us, you have no 'ego,' right, Perfect One?"

I realized at that moment that Devadatta was a true son of filth, so consumed with dark, irrational hatred for me that he would, before long, try to kill me. I would need to be on my guard against him from that point forward.

That night it was quite warm and Ananda was fanning me. After a moment: "The truth is that Devadatta has made *numerous* attempts to kill me in previous lifetimes, Ananda."

"That's terrible, master."

"Once, for instance, I was a large, beautiful monkey, a monkey-king, in fact, and Devadatta was a crocodile who wanted to eat me. (CMJAT) But do you know what I did, Ananda?"

"Tell me, master!"

"I jumped onto Devadatta's head and used it to leapfrog onto the opposite riverbank. Oh, he was quite upset by that, let me tell you, Ananda!"

"You outsmarted Devadatta by jumping on his head, master!"

"Yes, it was splendid."

"Are you going to do that again, master?"

"Am I going to do what again?"

"Jump on his head?"

"Am I going to jump on Devadatta's head? Why would I jump on Devadatta's head, Ananda?"

"Because . . . it worked so well in that other lifetime?"

"I was a *monkey* in that lifetime and Devadatta was a *crocodile!*"

"I'm so sorry, master." Ananda continued fanning me for a few minutes in silence. Then I continued.

"The fact is that Devadatta wants to BE me, Ananda. I think that's fairly obvious. And it's not the first time either. Once, in a different previous lifetime, I was a crow named Viraka and Devadatta was another crow who thought he could be just like me, but do you know what happened to that other crow, Ananda?" (MCJAT)

"He died, master?"

"Well, obviously he *died,* Ananda. The question is, do you know how?"

"Of old age?"

"He *drowned,* Ananda. And after he was dead, his wife asked me if I'd seen him."

"The Devadatta crow was married, master?"

"Yes, and when his wife asked if I'd seen him, this is what I said: 'The poor bird has found a watery grave.' Ha."

"Was Devadatta's wife upset, master?"

"Her husband had just died, so yes, Ananda, she was upset. She wept profusely, in fact."

"That is so sad."

"No, it is not sad, Ananda, it's not sad at *all.* Devadatta *deserved* it, he was trying to be like me so he died, just like he will before long in this lifetime." I took a sip of tea, nodded. "I think everyone in the *sangha* despises Devadatta and thinks him an arrogant fool, Ananda. I truly do."

"Other than his five hundred followers, you mean, master?"

"Devadatta's followers are despicable fools, walking bags of shit and piss, Ananda!" (UD 5:8)

"Yes, master, I'm so sorry, master."

A few more moments passed in silence, then Ananda said in a small voice: "Are you scared of Devadatta, master?"

I smiled indulgently. "Let me put it this way, Ananda: Is a *lion* scared?"

"Oh, definitely not."

"The lion fills *other* creatures with fear, Ananda. He forces them to hide in their holes or run away when he roars. Even elephants, even *elephants,* shit themselves when they see the lion, that is how fearsome he is."

". . . You are the lion, right, master?"

"*Obviously* I'm the lion, Ananda. I am fearsome to everyone:

Animals, humans, Hungry Ghosts, demigods, demons. I even frighten the *gods*, Ananda."

"That is amazing, master."

"When the gods hear my words they are filled with terror. 'But we thought we were *superior,* Tathagata.' 'Well, guess what, gods, you are *not.*'"

"Haha, stupid gods."

"No, Ananda, the gods are not stupid. They are simply ignorant, just like everyone else."

"Except you, master."

"Except me, Ananda, that is exactly right. As to your question: Am I scared of Devadatta? What do you think the answer is?"

". . . Yes?"

"I want you to understand something, Ananda. In the end you will be punished for this kind of remark."

22

But Devadatta did have a strange power over people, I cannot deny it. I later learned that he was a skilled hypnotist who mind-controlled many of his followers. I also later learned that he could shape-shift, that one time he turned himself into a man who wore a girdle made entirely of snakes, which was apparently quite disconcerting. (CV 7:2) In any case, his challenges against me continued; if anything, they intensified.

"Have you not instructed us to behave harmlessly towards all living things, Perfect One?" Devadatta asked one day. (DP 19)

"I have."

"Should we not therefore refrain from eating animals?" (CV 7:2–3)

"My instructions were to not 'harm' animals, Devadatta. I never said don't 'eat' them. If they're already dead and you merely eat them—well, no harm done."

"But wouldn't it be more *compassionate* to not eat animals at all, Perfect One?"

"I think we all agree that one should not eat tigers."

"No one eats tigers, Perfect One."

"Which is good, because we should not. Nor should we eat lions, hyenas or leopards."

"But again, no one eats lions, hyenas or leopards."

"Or bears, *definitely* don't eat bears. As for all the other animals, I repeat, as long as you don't kill them it is perfectly fine to eat them." (MV 6)

"But Perfect One—"

"Being a vegetarian is not what makes one 'good,' Devadatta. Understanding that life is pain, that is what makes one good."

As the lesson ended and the group broke up, I smiled thinly at Devadatta. "No snare like delusion, is there, *bikkhu*?"

"On that we agree, Perfect One."

"Easy to see in others, but much harder to see in oneself, eh?"

"Again, we agree. But I wonder, Perfect One: Is it not possible that the *ultimate* delusion might lie in thinking that one has achieved the ultimate enlightenment?"

"Ultimate enlightenment *precludes* delusion, Devadatta." He tried to speak but I talked right over him. "*Wake up, Devadatta. WAKE UP.*"

"Perhaps I am already awake, Perfect One."

"No, Devadatta, you are not. What you are, sadly, is a fish out of water, flopping around on the dry ground and honestly, not even worth eating. You are *Mara's* fish, Devadatta, a devil fish and not tasty in the least. (DP 3:34) A man whose mind is trained does not smell like dead fish the way you do, Devadatta, rather what that man smells like is—"

"Flowers, Perfect One?"

"Sandalwood flowers, to be specific, and let me assure you, Devadatta, the scent of enlightenment is *incomparable*." (DP 4:54–55)

That night, wanting to "nip things in the bud," I visited Devadatta in his chambers.

"I understand you well, cousin," I remember telling him. "You are, as you always have been, consumed with jealousy for me."

"Oh?"

"All you have ever wished for is to *be* me, Devadatta, it is quite obvious. In one previous lifetime after another, this has been the case. Once, for instance, I was a lion who befriended a jackal—" (JBJAT)

"The jackal was me, obviously."

"Yes. You said you wanted to serve me so I took you in and fed you but before long, do you know what happened, Devadatta?"

"I became proud?"

"Exactly so, you became proud. 'I can hunt an elephant just like you can, lion,' you boasted. 'Beware, jackal,' I warned you, 'you are but puny and no match for an elephant.' But did you listen to me?"

"I think I did not."

"Correct, you did not. You tried to jump on an elephant's head but you missed, landed at its feet and were instantly crushed. You laid there moaning in pain for a while and then you died. Do you know what I said at that point, Devadatta?"

"Something compassionate, I would think?"

"I recited a kind of poem."

"How deep."

"Here it is:

> *A jackal assumed a lion's pride*
> *Now he's prone, now he's died*
> *Now his rashness he repents*
> *Jackal's worthless life is spent.*"

"It's so moving."

"Do not challenge those bigger than you, Devadatta, that is what I was trying to tell the jackal, because you will be *crushed*."

"I find it interesting that I have no memory of this lifetime whatsoever, Perfect One."

"Perhaps you remember the lifetime in which you were a cruel elephant who had its eyes pecked out by a crow?" (SYEJAT)

"It sounds memorably painful, but no, I don't."

"You don't remember the fly laying *eggs* in your empty eye sockets and causing you to fall off a cliff?"

"I don't, actually."

"Well, I am certain you recall this lifetime, Devadatta: I was a monkey-king named Jolly who lived with his younger brother, Jollikins, and—"

"I'm sorry, Perfect One, but did you just say your name was 'Jolly' and your younger brother's name was 'Jollikins'?" (JTMKJAT)

"Yes, and we lived with our blind mother. One day, however, an extremely evil man showed up in the forest."

"That would be me."

"It certainly would be. You were a cruel, vindictive and ugly man."

"That is not surprising to hear."

"You wanted to eat our blind mother, so Jollikins and I sacrificed ourselves, but it did not matter because you killed us all anyway."

"Well, success for me, I guess."

"No, Devadatta, NOT success for you, not in the least. At the *very* moment that you killed us, lightning hit your house, killing your entire family and then when you got home the house fell on your head and crushed you!"

"What a reversal of fortune."

"After that the earth opened up, *swallowed* you and deposited you straight into Hell, Devadatta."

"I find it fascinating that I don't recall any of these lifetimes, Perfect One."

"This final one I am quite sure you will remember, Devadatta. Does a white elephant ring a bell?" (OEJAT)

Devadatta's eyes suddenly widened. "Perhaps I *do* remember this lifetime, Perfect One. Was the white elephant beautiful?"

"Extremely."

"Did his eyes sparkle like diamonds?"

"Yes."

"Did his feet gleam like polished lacquer?"

"They definitely did."

"Did everyone love him?"

"Except for one person, the evil King."

"Who was *jealous* of you, wasn't he, Perfect One?"

"Yes. So much so that he (you) tried to get me to walk off a cliff, Devadatta. And do you know what, I *did it* too. But there was something you did not realize about me."

"You could *fly,* couldn't you, Perfect One?"

"That's exactly right, I could fly. I was a flying elephant who, in the end, became the emperor of India."

"That is remarkable because elephants aren't usually made the emperor of India, Perfect One."

"No, Devadatta, they are not, but I was."

"I should listen more carefully to your words, shouldn't I, Perfect One?"

"Yes, Devadatta, you should."

"But oh, before you go, may I ask *you* one question?"

"You may."

"Would you say it was 'perfect' on your part to walk out on my sister and nephew, your newborn son?"

I gazed coolly back at him, shook my head. "I find it sad that you *still* seem not to grasp that I had a *world* to save, Devadatta, a universe perhaps. Your sister was thinking only of herself, wanting her beautiful husband with his perfect body and his magnificent mind to stay with her. But this was self-involved. We are not meant to think of ourselves in that way, do you still not grasp that, Devadatta?"

"To be clear then, walking out on your family *was* 'perfect'?"

We stared at each for a moment, then I spoke: "I am sorry to have to say this, Devadatta, but you are a degenerate and you are not welcome in my *sangha* anymore." And with that, I turned and exited his tent.

Not long afterwards the murder attempts began.

23

Devadatta's first attempt on my life started off simply: He ordered a man to kill me. Quickly, however, his plot got bizarrely complicated. To cover up *my* murder, Devadatta ordered two men to kill the first man. To cover up *that* murder, he ordered *four* men to kill the two, then eight men to kill the four and sixteen men to kill the eight. When I heard about this plan, I shook my head in disbelief. "It's the stupidest idea of all time," I remember thinking. "If Devadatta keeps hiring killers to kill other killers, before long he'll have a thousand killers killing five hundred killers!" It didn't matter, however, because when the first killer showed up to murder me, he instantly grew frightened. "Don't be scared," I reassured him. "I am pure love and compassion." Before long my spotless vision had converted him. Before long, in fact, I had converted all thirty-one of Devadatta's assassins! (CV 7:3–4)

After this initial failure, Devadatta decided to take things into his own hands. He climbed to the top of Vulture Rock, waited for me to pass by, then hurled a stone down at me. (Why Devadatta thought I was so feeble that a thrown *rock* could kill me I still do not know.) The rock did not kill me, obviously, but a shard of it did hit my foot, drawing a bit of blood. That offended me deeply. I glared up at Devadatta and screamed, "You have drawn the blood of a Perfect One!" I then turned to Ananda and told him the same thing: "Devadatta has drawn the blood of a Perfect One!"

That night, my foot hurt so badly that it kept me awake. For some reason, Mara chose that moment to reappear. "Why are you lying down, monk?" he jeered. "Don't you have better things to do than *rest*?" "I rest out of compassion for all living things, Mara," I instantly shot back and, as always, he instantly deflated and slouched away in defeat. (SY 4:13) I would have to say that I was fortunate in my adversaries. Mara was a witless blowhard; all he ever did was make bombastic threats, then leave as soon as I told him to. Devadatta turned out to be similarly feckless. If he wanted me dead so much, why didn't he just sneak up on me while I was asleep and cut my throat? His plans were both convoluted and idiotic.

That said, I will acknowledge that Devadatta's third attempt on my life was genuinely terrifying. Devadatta went to the stable where Nalagiri, the man-killing elephant, was kept and bribed Nalagiri's keepers to let the elephant loose just as I was strolling past. When Nalagiri saw me, he instantly charged, his trunk raised, his tail straight out. "Look out, master!" Ananda cried. "Nalagiri the killer elephant wants to kill you, run away!"

Did I run away? No, I calmly stood my ground. "When a Perfect One reaches *nirvana*, it is never through violence, Ananda," I coolly announced. I heard people screaming: "That handsome man is going to be stomped by that killer elephant!" I appreciated the compliment about my looks, but the lack of faith in me was slightly irksome. As the crazed behemoth rumbled closer, Ananda trembled with fear. "*Master?*" he whispered. Nalagiri was nearly on us now. I briefly considered popping him in the ear, because that does sometimes work (DP 23), but instead I decided to raise my hands up and hold them palm out, sending powerful beams of loving-kindness directly at Nalagiri. Instantly affected by my compassion, the massive elephant slowed, and then stopped directly in front of me. He bowed his mighty head to me. "*Blessed One,*" I saw in his great eyes. (CV 7:3)

"You were working for Devadatta, weren't you, tusker?" I asked Nalagiri silently.

"Yes, Tathagata. Devadatta is consumed with jealousy for you, as I'm sure you already know."

"Oh yes."

"I am ashamed of myself, master."

"Do not be ashamed, dear tusker. I forgive you."

At this, Nalagiri dropped to his knees before me and gazed up at me with profound gratitude. "I love you, Blessed One," I saw in his eyes.

"I love you too, tusker," I told him silently, gently patting his enormous head. "But in that spirit I must tell you that it is now time for you to give up lust, anger and delusion."

"I will, Perfect One, I promise. Please, may I join your *sangha*?"

"I am sorry, beloved tusker, but as you are an elephant, no, you may not."

At that point, having failed for the third time to kill me, Devadatta tried to take over the *sangha*. You would *think* he'd have tried to take over the *sangha* first and *then* tried to kill me, that definitely would have been more logical, but as I said, Devadatta's plans never made a whole lot of sense. I remember vividly the day Devadatta openly attacked my leadership. "The Perfect One has been leading us for many years now," he loudly announced. "Perhaps it is time for him to rest and enjoy his remaining days, allowing someone else to lead the *sangha*. With that in mind, I humbly offer myself."

There was something about the unctuous way Devadatta said these words that made me suddenly explode with emotion. "Do you actually think I would allow a clot of spittle like *you* to lead my *sangha*, Devadatta??" I bellowed. "Never! NEVER!"

That night at bedtime, Ananda trimmed my toenails. "I am slightly saddened about what I suspect Devadatta's fate is going to be, Ananda." (ITI 89)

"Is it going to be terrible, master?"

"It's going to be very terrible indeed, my friend. Devadatta will go to Hell, where he will be forced to embrace a flaming metal pillar which will burn all of his flesh off, thus turning him into a skeleton."

"Oh no!"

"His skeleton will then be brought back to life."

"Dreadful!"

"And forced to hug *another* fiery pillar, which will turn him into a skeleton once again. His skeleton will then be tossed into a fire and pulled out and thrown in again, over and over and over." (NRK)

"It sounds excruciating, master."

"Oh yes, Ananda, extremely excruciating. The point is, one may *not* criticize a Buddha, Ananda." (SDI)

"No no."

"Anyone who does—well, how to put it? 'For eons he will be born to a whore who will abandon him to wild dogs.'" (NRK)

"Will the wild dogs eat Devadatta, master?"

"What *else* would they do with him, Ananda?"

". . . Raise him?"

"Of *course* they will eat him, you nincompoop!"

"I'm so sorry, master."

That night I dreamed of a previous lifetime. I was the captain of a great sailing ship who at one point on a long sea voyage knew with psychic certainty that one of my passengers was planning to kill all of the other passengers. (CCJAT) Why this passenger wanted to kill five hundred people, I did not know. Why all the other passengers would simply *allow* themselves to be killed by this one man, I did not know either. All I knew was that as captain of the ship, I had only one choice: Kill the murderer before he could kill anyone else. I remember the moment I snuck up behind the man and stuck my knife in his back. He jerked around, looked at me and whispered, "But Captain, what did I even *do*?" "Nothing yet," I whispered to him, "but you soon would have. I have saved you from Hell, my friend, and you are welcome."

"But master," Ananda asked me the next morning when I told him of my dream, "is not our commitment to do no harm?"

"It is, Ananda, but it turns out that sometimes the best way to do no harm is to kill someone."

"Did the man on the ship die quickly, master?"

"No, Ananda, I'm afraid it took several minutes for him to bleed out. 'My family,' I remember him gurgling up at me. 'Do not even think about them, friend,' I responded. 'They were nothing but shackles on you anyway. Think instead of how I have freed you from Hell and again, you are welcome.'"

A few moments later: "How would you kill Devadatta, master?"

"I'm not entirely sure, Ananda, but I am seriously considering getting Nalagiri the killer elephant to stomp him to death. I am also considering pushing him off a cliff."

It turned out that there was no need for me to kill Devadatta, however. Once Sariputta, Moggallana and I lured Devadatta's five hundred followers away from him (which turned out to be easy because they were all nitwits), that was effectively the end for Devadatta. The next day he started vomiting up blood. "Devadatta will die in *agony*," I informed Ananda that night. "Vomiting up blood is just the beginning. Devadatta will now experience prolonged *misery*." (CV 7:4)

Shortly after that, the earth opened up beneath Devadatta's feet and swallowed him whole. (SY 3:14–15) I found this to be a rather abrupt conclusion to his story. I wished Devadatta's death had been somewhat more drawn out, like if crows with metal beaks had slowly pecked him to death or he had slowly drowned in a vat of his own feces. Still, I did comfort myself with the knowledge that immediately afterwards, Devadatta was (and is to this very day I assume) impaled on a fiery iron pillar in Hell.

Had I been physically present when Devadatta died, I would have spoken the following words: "You have behaved badly, cousin, you have tried to obstruct the Buddha. Because of this, you will now go to Hell." "I understand, Perfect One," Devadatta would have groaned in response. "I confess my wickedness to you and beseech you to forgive me. I praise you boundlessly, Perfect One, and seek refuge in your loving, compassionate eyes." "I am afraid it is too late for that, Devadatta, now it is time for you to burn forever, farewell."

part 3: end

24

Now I will tell you about the final months of my life.

I was old, over eighty years of age, living near Vulture Rock. I had decided that, much as I yearned for extinction, it would be better for the world if I lived on, not *forever* exactly, but close to it. In order for this to happen, Ananda had to ask me, *beg* me really, to continue living. Why things were set up that way, I have no idea. But I started dropping hints. (LSV 2; MPB)

One day Ananda and I were on top of Robber's Cliff. I glanced over at him and sort of offhandedly remarked, "What a lovely place Robber's Cliff is, eh, Ananda?" "Oh yes, master, very lovely indeed." "Did you know, Ananda, that a being who has attained the very heights of awareness, has become a saint, essentially, did you know that such a being could live on for literally *eons* if he was only asked to? Isn't that fascinating?" Ananda stared back at me in smiling silence. "Live on, Blessed One!" he was supposed to instantly cry out. "For the good of all the world, LIVE ON!" If he had said that, I was going to refuse him at first and make him repeat his plea, then refuse him again, and only when he had asked me for the *third* time, accept. But Ananda didn't say a word. He just yawned and looked away.

I tried a second time a few weeks later at Serpent's Pool. "What a grand place Serpent's Pool is, eh, Ananda? Say, did I ever mention to you that a being who has fully awakened, a being like *me*, that is, could live on for, well, pretty much *forever* if only someone like YOU begged him to do so, did I mention that, Ananda?" Once again Ananda only gazed back at me and smiled blankly. I stepped things up at that point and started dropping hints everywhere we went, at Sattapani Cave, at Black Rock, even at the Squirrels' Feeding Ground. "How pleasant this place is, eh, Ananda?" I would invariably begin. "Have I ever mentioned, old friend, that when a being *like me* has ascended to the very heights of perfection he could live on for a VERY long time if he was only asked to by another person, like *you*?"

But every single time Ananda only nodded vaguely and smiled back at me. Not only did he not *beg* me to stay, he never even *asked* me to. "Why do I require this dunce of an assistant to ask me to live on, why can't I just do it myself?" I remember fuming on more than one occasion. Finally one night I got so fed up with Ananda's obliviousness that I barked, "Get out of my tent!" at him. Ananda hustled to his feet, saluted me, and exited. I sat there grinding my teeth for a few minutes, then closed my eyes to meditate, took a few deep breaths—and felt someone standing right next to me. "Time to *die*, Buddha," I heard a voice whispering in my ear. Opening my eyes, I saw Mara squatting next to me, smiling maliciously and twirling his moustache. I found this extremely irritating. I was *not* going to be told what to do by this jackass. "I will *not* die, Mara," I replied, "until my followers are ready."

"But your followers *are* ready," Mara quickly countered. "I repeat: Time to die."

Once again, I shook my head dismissively. "I will not die until my religion has become a success, Mara."

"But your religion *has* become a success. So for the third time I tell you: *Time to die*." (ANG 8:70)

I stared at Mara, not totally sure what to say next; he'd actually made some valid points for once. "Given that my entire life I have been extolling 'extinction,' the fact that I am fighting so hard to stay alive at this point is vaguely ironic," I remember thinking to myself. "Fine," I finally growled at Mara, "in three months I will die, *satisfied?*" Mara gaped back at me, apparently so accustomed to failing in my presence that he was rendered speechless by this success. I decided to confuse him further by singing a little song about myself in third person.

The rest of his life Tathagata's renounced.
With joy and calm, life's cause he's denounced!

Mara got up and wandered away at that point, looking puzzled and insecure; my song had obviously rattled him.

Ananda came rushing back in. "What caused that massive earthquake, master?" he asked breathlessly. (Because there had been a huge earthquake when I announced that I would die in three months.) I was still furious with Ananda for not begging me to live on but this was undeniably a valid question. "There were numerous causes to the earthquake, Ananda," I began. "First of all, as a purely scientific matter, earth rests upon water, which rests upon wind, which rests upon space. Therefore when the winds blow, that makes the water move, which shakes the earth."

"I see, thank you, master."

"But there is a second, deeper answer to your question, Ananda," I continued. "Earthquakes, you see, occur at six key moments in human life. First, when a Buddha is conceived; second, when a Buddha is born; third, when a Buddha is enlightened; fourth, when a Buddha begins to teach; fifth, when a Buddha chooses to die; sixth, when a Buddha actually *does* die. Does that answer your question, my friend?" (UD 6:1; MPB)

"Are you dead, master?"

"Am I—? No, Ananda, I'm not dead, I have *decided* to die and soon, in three months, I will be dead."

Ananda shook his head in disbelief. "Don't say that, master, no no no, you must *live on,* for the good of the entire world, you must live for EONS!"

"I'm afraid it is too late for that now, Ananda."

"Master, please! You must live on, oh truly you must!"

At that point I'd had enough. "If you think that, Ananda, then why didn't you beg me to live on *earlier,* hm?"

"What do you mean, master?"

"I made it *obvious* that you needed to beg me to stay, Ananda. Why didn't you do it?"

"But . . . I am asking you, master."

"Yes, but it's too late now."

"Why, master?"

"I don't *know* why, it just is. You needed to do it *earlier,* Ananda, and you missed your chance!"

"Oh, master, *no!*"

"If you'd been persistent, Ananda, if you'd begged me three times, I would have stayed for eons!"

"Master, *please* . . ."

"I'm sorry to have to say this, old friend, but it is *your* fault that I am going to die."

"Oh noooooooooo . . ."

"I gave you the most *overt* hints, Ananda, at Vulture Rock, near Serpent's Pool, even in the Squirrels' Feeding Ground, I practically spelled things out for you but you just stood there like a big dummy every single time and now I'm going to die and, yes, it is ALL YOUR FAULT!" (ANG 4:1)

At that point Ananda collapsed to the ground and started to weep. His body shook and shuddered through his terrible sobs. After a long moment, I sighed and spoke to him in a softer voice. "Everything dies, Ananda, that is the nature of existence, you know that. In three months, the Buddha will die, that too is natural." Ananda stared up at me, eyes brimming with tears. "Now get up, old friend," I said to him. "I have many people to talk to before I leave this world."

25

"I will have the pig's delight," I announced to Kunda, the man whose home we were staying in a few nights later. The pig's delight, when it arrived, was delicious, quite savory, one of the very best pig's delights I'd ever had. When some of my monks glanced over at me as I ate, I addressed them in no uncertain terms: "No one will eat this pig's delight but the Tathagata!"

After I finished my meal, I remember sitting back and wondering if there was anything that would make the leftover pig's delight taste even *better*? An answer occurred to me: What if Kunda buried the remaining pig's delight in a pit for a while, "aged" it, mightn't that make it taste even more delicious? I thought it might. "Bury this leftover pig's delight, my good man," I instructed Kunda. (MPB 4:18–20) "The next time we are back here," I remember thinking to myself as he exited the room with my bowl, "I have a feeling that my pig's delight is going to be absolutely *scrummy*."

Later that night I noticed Ananda looking over at me with a concerned expression on his face. "What is it, old friend?"

"I am worried that the pig's delight you ate was tainted, master."

I waved my hand dismissively. "Fear not, old friend. The Tathagata has a superb digestive system, everything he eats is digested with perfect ease."

"That is a relief to hear, master, because that pig's delight looked, to be honest, slightly rotten."

"Let me clarify something for you, Ananda. The Tathagata *chews* perfectly, the Tathagata *swallows* perfectly and the Tathagata *digests* perfectly."

"That is wonderful to hear, master."

"The Tathagata never gets sick, Ananda, and this is why: Because the Tathagata has *transcended* sickness." (AVDS)

"Oh, good."

Sadly, however, Ananda turned out to be right; the pig's delight I'd eaten had been rotten. I woke up in the middle of the night with violent, bloody diarrhea. (UD 8:5; MPB) "I'm going to defecate myself to death," I remember quickly grasping. That was *not* the exit I would have liked, to say the very least. "Shitting myself out" seemed highly undignified. (I'd kind of thought that I would eventually turn into a solid piece of gold, to be honest.) (SV) On the positive side, however, I would have looked like a fool if I'd guaranteed Mara that I was going to die in three months and then hadn't done it. I needed *something* to "take me out," and looked at that way, the tainted pig's delight was a godsend. (If I hadn't been poisoned, did I have a "back-up plan" to end my life? Yes. I was going to throw myself under Nalagiri the killer elephant.)

Q: Did I blame Kunda, the man who had served me the rotten pig's delight, for my dysentery? A: No, I certainly did not. "If anyone should *ever* hold Kunda responsible for my death," I instructed Ananda the next morning, "if anyone should *ever* refer to him as 'Buddha-killer' or 'Destroyer of Perfection,' or anything like that, you must immediately correct them, Ananda. 'No,' you must tell them, 'it is *good* that Kunda caused the Perfect One's death, because it helped him achieve extinction. For this, Kunda is not to be criticized, but rather *praised*. The truth is that Kunda should be rich, famous and, honestly, good-looking for killing the Perfect One!'" (MPB 4:42) At that moment, feeling emotional, I began to sing.

To the good comes the good
To the bad comes the bad
I feel no anger, I am not sad
I am not bitter, I feel no lust
Soon I will be merely bones, merely dust.

Later that day I rested on one side, catching my breath between bouts of diarrhea. Ananda sat next to me, holding my hand. As I winced, he squeezed my hand. "Shall I sing to you of your many marvelous qualities, master?"

"That would be very nice, Ananda," I whispered.

Ananda had a deep, gravelly singing voice, not exactly good but definitely sincere. *"Morning star, oh man of love, Holy One came from above,"* he began.

"Lovely . . ."

"Always good and always true, like a glorious sky of blue. Lotus man, no Lotus King, you know literally everything!"

"It's true . . ."

"Like an angel is this man, who can best him, no one can! Exalted Being, Incomparable Soul, utter extinction is your goal!"

"Well done, Ananda, thank you, my UUUHHHHHHHHH." I stopped, unable to continue because of the pain. A few moments later, Ananda looked at me with an unsure expression on his face. "Master?"

"Hm?"

"Is it true that *another* Buddha, named 'Maitreya,' is already in heaven, getting ready to enter the world and teach us?"

"Who said that?"

"I have heard various townspeople talking about it. Some of them are praying to be reborn when Maitreya arrives, others are using alchemy to extend their lives so that they might meet him."

"These people are delusional, Ananda."

"They say his name means 'Kindness,' master. They believe

that he will be exceedingly kind and good-hearted, jovial even."

"Enough about this made-up character, 'Maitreya.' I need to rest, Ananda."

"Yes, master, I'm so sorry, master."

26

That night I had a vivid dream. I was flying over the world in a wooden boat. Hearing a slight giggle, I turned to my left. A fat, shirtless man sat there, grinning back at me as he guided the flying boat. "Who are you?" I whispered.

"Do you not know me, Tathagata?" the man chuckled, his great belly jiggling as he did.

"Are you the one called 'Maitreya'?"

"Indeed I am, Tathagata, the very one, hahahahaha!"

"What are you laughing about?"

"I am jolly, Tathagata, for many reasons, but in part because I am thrilled to see my half-brother!"

"We are not half-brothers."

"Oh, but we are! Maya is my mother too! (GV 44) Also, I bear wonderful news!"

"What do you mean?"

"Look down, my friend!"

I did and saw that we were flying over the Ganges. "First the bad news, Tathagata. Your lovely little religion is going to fail utterly here in your homeland. There are several reasons for this: Hinduism, which you have stolen so much from (hahaha, just kidding—*dharma*, *karma*, *reincarnation*, *meditation*, these are only TINY little lifts, right?), will reassert itself. Then later, a whole new religion will appear from the west, Tathagata, expressing a belief in one god who rules over absolutely *everything*. 'Allah,' they will call him, and between these two, Hinduism and what will be called 'Islam,' your charming little religion will be swept away completely, Tathagata, oh boohoo! But not to worry, my friend, because now we get to the *wonderful* news! Your religion, you see, will simply move north—NOW you will understand why I look the way I do—into *China*!"

Suddenly the flying boat zoomed up and over the Himalayas and in the blink of an eye we were cruising over a landscape I had never seen before.

"Your religion will *flourish* in China, Tathagata!" Maitreya announced. "Here they will grasp things about your teachings that no one ever had before!"

"Like what?"

"Like the existence of Pure Land, for instance!"

"Pure Land? What are you talking about?"

"Hahaha, you are so funny, Tathagata! Pure Land, where one lives in *eternal bliss* after death!"

"I never said anything about the existence of such a place. What I said was that life is pain and the only relief from that pain is *extinction*. I have literally never said *one word* about a place called 'Pure Land.'"

Maitreya smiled a sly little smile and spoke in an insinuating voice which I instantly despised. "Oh, but people were onto you, Tathagata, they knew what you *really* meant. After you are dead (and it won't be long now, my friend, that pig's delight is doing its work on you as we speak, haha), lessons will emerge in which you reveal your *real* meaning! You didn't achieve 'enlightenment' at the age of thirty-five, you were enlightened the whole time, you were just being clever!" (LOT) Then, before I could respond, Maitreya cried out, "Hold on, Clever One!" and we shot forward again, this time zooming across the ocean. As we approached a large island, he nodded. "Here is *another* place where your religion will take hold, Tathagata. Supreme wisdom here in Japan will be realized through asking questions such as the following: 'What is the sound of one hand clapping?'"

" . . . What?"

"What is the sound—?"

"It doesn't make any sense, one hand can't possibly—"

Maitreya casually reached over and slapped me in the face, hard.

"What was that for?"

"*That* is how future students will be taught in Japan, Tathagata!"

"By being *hit*?"

"It will lead them to sudden awakening! Here's another excellent question for you: 'What *is* the Buddha?'"

"I don't . . ."

"A dried shit stick!" Maitreya cried merrily and once again hit me in the face with his meaty hand. (CSG)

"I am certainly not a dried shit stick and *stop hitting me.*"

"Now the *real* excitement begins, Tathagata, hold on tight!" Maitreya exclaimed and with that, we suddenly exploded straight upward at a dazzling speed. The moon, the stars and the planets whizzed by us in a sort of mad blur before, just as suddenly as we took off, we slowed down. We were now floating lazily over an almost indescribably beautiful landscape, green and verdant, laced with burbling, limpid streams and dotted with magnificently vibrant flowers and trees.

"Where *are* we?" I gasped.

"Welcome to Pure Land, Tathagata. Breathtaking, isn't it?!" As we drifted slowly over a magnificent forest: "The trees here do not bear fruit, Tathagata, rather they bear *jewels*!" (LSV 16)

"That doesn't make any sense, you can't eat jewels."

"Ah, but the beings who live in Pure Land *do* eat jewels, Tathagata. They LOVE eating jewels, that's how refined they are! They don't eat revolting things like *gravy*, oh no no. No one here would *ever* wish for gravy, the truth is they wouldn't be here in Pure Land if they did, hahahaha! (LSV 19) Because they eat jewels, there are no horrible ailments in Pure Land.

There are no retards, no hunchbacks, no cripples, and as for st-st-st-stammering, it simply does not exist. Isn't that wonderful?" (PMKS 228–57)

Now we floated over a grove of tall, thin, perfectly straight trees. "Those are the wishing trees, Tathagata! All you need to do is *wish* for something from them and you will receive it! Go ahead, my friend, wish for something, anything! A giant diamond perhaps? A massive pearl? A lapis lazuli necklace? Your wish will be fulfilled, whatever it is, I assure you!"

"As I told you, all I wish for is extinction."

"Oh no no no, Tathagata, that is *far* too negative! Pure Land is a place of endless happiness and joy!" (NBS)

"Happiness and joy do not even *exist*. All that exists is pain."

"How funny you are, Tathagata, how very droll, hahahaha!" Maitreya now steered the flying wooden boat over a vibrant little town where beaming people in brightly colored outfits skipped joyfully about. "Welcome to *Amithaba* City, Tathagata!"

"Who is Amithaba?"

"Amithaba is the beloved ruler of Pure Land, Tathagata! Soon you will meet him, *very* exciting."

Before I could respond, Maitreya nodded excitedly. "Look at all the charming stores, Tathagata! They sell musical instruments—flags ... umbrellas ... jewelry ... perfumes! Everything a person needs to be eternally happy, wouldn't you say? Look at all the splendid banners!" Looking down, I could see people marching around, carrying banners that read things like, "WE LOVE AMITHABA!" or "HOORAY FOR AMITHABA!" "They are having a parade in honor of their beloved leader!" Maitreya cocked his head slightly. "Listen, Tathagata, even the *gods* are cheering for them now! And oh my goodness, LOOK! Some of the gods are dancing with them, isn't that captivating? What a blissful place Pure Land is, eh, Tathagata? All those people and gods dancing and playing trumpets and shaking their jewelry around, this is the true *nirvana*, isn't it, my friend?" (LSV 19–26; PMKS 228–57)

Again, before I could respond: "And look at all the happy children, Tathagata! In case you are wondering, by the way, yes, they will stay children *indefinitely*! No one ages here in Pure Land, there is no birth, no death and certainly no *sex* (that part I know you will approve of, *hahahahahaha!*). Look how the children's jewelry sparkles! Do you know how many jewels each child's necklace contains, Tathagata? Five hundred *million*! That's a lot of jewels, isn't it? (BA 12) The gods all have perfect penises, incidentally." (LSV 35)

"...What did you just say?"

"Perfect penises, the gods all have them, as I'm sure you know."

Now we suddenly passed through a thick cloud of flowers. "It's raining flowers, Tathagata, isn't it glorious? Look at all the beautiful birds down on the ground. Six times a day they perform a *concert*, singing about virtue and wisdom and also of course praising our beloved leader, Amithaba! (SSV 6) And listen to that stream, Tathagata! It's making music too, do you hear? The stream's song is discussing the nature of suffering. How very profound! *Look,* Tathagata, musical instruments are floating all around us, playing along with the stream's melancholy tune! How utterly breathtaking!" (LSV 23; BA 14)

We headed towards what looked like an endless, perfectly circular lake covered with gigantic flowers. "Now we get to the most important part of Pure Land, Tathagata: The giant lotus flowers! These flowers, in case you are wondering, are one hundred miles wide! Out of the center of each one of them shoot *trillions* of rays of light, and from each individual ray of light emerges—you will like this, Tathagata—three thousand seven hundred *golden Buddhas*!! Look at all the golden Buddhas popping out of the giant lotus flowers, they seem *virtually infinite*, don't they?" (LSV 16)

It was true, the sky around us was suddenly thick with flying golden Buddhas. "This is a dream," I murmured to myself. "It is literally not *possible* for there to be so many Buddhas."

"Oh, and why not, Tathagata?"

"The appearance of a *single* Buddha is a momentous occasion in the history of the universe."

"Agreed!"

"If even a *second* Buddha were to appear, the entire universe would collapse."

"Oh no no no!"

"A Buddha requires ALL of the universe's resources to sustain his brief and shining presence and therefore there cannot possibly be *trillions* of them, it is absurd." (MQ; LOT)

"But look at all the golden Buddhas flying around! And here's a fun fact: Eventually *everyone* will be a Buddha and do you know why? Because everyone possesses *Buddha Nature!*"

"No, **I** am the only Buddha."

"Indeed you are, Tathagata! But not for much longer, haha!" Then, in a hushed, reverent voice: "Look, Tathagata, *it is Amithaba.*"

There, at the center of the largest lotus flower of them all, dead center of the giant lake, sat a motionless figure, dressed all in white. As we glided silently towards him: "All you need to do to come live here in Pure Land and exist in eternal pleasure is say his name, Tathagata." Maitreya whispered. "On your deathbed, merely say, '*Amithaba . . . Amithaba . . . Amithaba,*' and he will guide you here to Pure Land, if you are lucky on his boat of love, 'Najrayana,' which means 'Diamond Thunderbolt Vehicle.' Isn't that spectacular?" (LSV 28; OJO, Pure Land)

"No, it's pretentious."

"Remember, Tathagata—'*Amithaba . . . Amithaba . . . Amithaba.*'"

Then, in a flash I was standing at the center of the giant lotus flower, facing Amithaba. He sat cross-legged with his eyes closed. I looked around; Maitreya was gone. Without opening his eyes, Amithaba spoke. "I am Amithaba," he proclaimed. "I welcome you to my home, the true *nirvana,* Pure Land.*"

"This is a dream."

"Do you wish to stay here in Pure Land, sinner?"

"Of course I don't wish to stay here in Pure Land."

"I, Amithaba, hold the sole key to existence. Behold me, sinner, bow down before me and be saved."

"I will not."

"Bow down in humility and I will save you."

"This is a nightmare . . ."

Amithaba's eyes popped open and he stared directly into my eyes. "All the goodness of the universe is gathered in *my* name," he said. "Speak my name now, sinner."

"I will not."

"Speak my name and surrender to me, sinner, *surrender to me NOW.*"

"NO."

"Say '*Amithaba . . . Amithaba . . . Amithaba . . .*'"

"NOOOOOOOOOOOOOOOOOOOOOOOOOOOOOOOOOOOOOOOOO!"

I woke up in a cold sweat. "In hindsight, I really shouldn't have eaten that pig's delight," I remember thinking.

27

"When you are gone, master, what will become of us, who will *lead* us?" Ananda asked two nights before my death.

"My ideas will continue to lead you, Ananda."

"Some of the monks have been asking questions, master. 'Why did the Tathagata not appoint a successor?' they say."

"What do you tell them, Ananda?"

"'How could *anyone* replace such a supremely enlightened being? The Perfect One's gaze is penetrating, his ideas are *unprecedented* and his beauty is *indescribable*. How dare you ask such a question?'"

"That is good."

"'The Tathagata is the flower of all mankind, a beautiful gem of many facets who cannot possibly be replaced, that is why he left us no successor.'"

"Exactly right, Ananda. Well done."

"'But why should not the Tathagata's *son* lead us?' some of the monks have asked."

"What's that?"

"'Rahula is not his father, monks,'" I tell them.

"Not even *close*."

"'But what about *you*, Ananda?' some of the monks have said. 'Why don't you lead us? After all, you have been with the Tathagata for over forty years now.'"

"You cannot possibly be the leader, Ananda."

"That is what I told them, master."

"Good . . . Good." (MPB 4)

Near bedtime, I glanced over at Ananda, who was staring back at me with a troubled look on his face. "You have something else you need to speak to me about, old friend?" I inquired gently.

"I need your guidance, master."

"I am listening, my friend."

Ananda crossed and sat at my feet. He hesitated for a moment, then spoke in a hectic rush. "As I have been begging in the nearby village, master, I have seen a woman numerous times and this woman has been quite generous with me, she has invited me into her home, even offered me tea, she is very kind and soft-spoken, master, and curious too, she has asked me about the *sangha*, about *dharma* and *nirvana*, and I have answered her and that is alright, isn't it, master, isn't it alright?"

Tears welled in Ananda's eyes. He was obviously desperately in need of spiritual guidance. "You have fallen under this woman's spell, I think, haven't you, old friend?" I said softly, patting his hand.

"I think I have, master, yes."

"And that is because she is a witch."

"A witch . . . ?"

"You have been weak, Ananda, but that is not your fault, because this witch has been weakening you."

"So . . . may I not continue visiting with her, master?"

"No, Ananda, you must avoid this witch completely."

"But what if I *do* see her?"

"Ignore her completely. Do not even acknowledge her."

"What if she speaks to *me*?"

"Walk past her like you do not even *hear* her, treat her like she does not even exist, like she is invisible." (MPB 5:9)

"But master—"

"I have told you this again and again, Ananda: Women are crocodiles in the river of life, do you still not grasp that?"

"I have come to *know* this woman, master, and I don't believe she *is* a witch, or a crocodile either. I cannot help but feel that she and I are both human beings, master, that we are somehow *alike*, that we might even in some sense *help* each other."

I stared at Ananda in silence for a long moment until he suddenly cracked. "Oh, I am so weak, master! In spite of all your magnificent teachings, this harlot has bewitched me."

"Everything will be alright now, Ananda."

"Women are so horribly evil, aren't they, master?"

"Yes, Ananda, they certainly are."

"I feel so *defiled* by this witch, so *corrupted*. Will I ever achieve *nirvana*, master?"

"It may take an *extremely* long time, Ananda, hundreds of billions of years, possibly even trillions, but eventually, yes, I think you will."

I heard Ananda weeping softly as I drifted off to sleep.

The next day we were on the move again. While I was near death, understand that I still maintained many of my "magical abilities." That day, for example, because I felt quite thirsty, I asked Ananda to get me some water. (I was extremely dehydrated by this time, as you might imagine, due to my violent, bloody diarrhea.) As the only water nearby was a stagnant little pool that had collected along the side of the road, Ananda shook his head. "This water is dirty, master. If you can wait a bit longer, we will be at the river." "*Bring me water NOW, Ananda,*" I insisted. Ananda turned back to the muddy little pool and gasped in shock when he saw that it had turned perfectly clear and bright. (MPB 4:24) Not long after that, more magic: We were standing on the edge of the river, wanting to cross it but with no way of doing so. I waved my arms around and suddenly—we were on the other side! (UD 8:5–6; MV 6:29) Ananda looked at me, stunned. I felt so pleased about this moment that I broke into song:

I am the Perfect One
Vibrant as a perfect sun

I am the Perfect One
Very soon my life is done!

"Master?" Ananda whispered to me later that night.

"Hm?"

"I have been wondering—have you and I shared previous lifetimes together?"

I smiled warmly over at him. "Of course we have, Ananda."

"And have I *aided* you, master?"

"Indeed you have, old friend." With an effort, I went up one elbow and looked at him.

"Once I was a sprite who lived in a forest, Ananda. Near where I lived there was a Wishing Tree, within which another sprite lived. I and that other sprite were great friends." (WTJAT)

"Was I the other sprite, master?"

"You were, Ananda."

"Oh I am so very happy."

"After a time, however, your Wishing Tree was cut down, Ananda."

"Oh no!"

"Yes, you were extremely sad about it. But do you know who saved you?"

"...You, master?"

"I tricked the humans and saved your Wishing Tree, isn't that wonderful, Ananda?"

"Yes, I mean . . . I was kind of hoping that I had helped *you,* master."

I patted his hand tenderly. "Let me tell you about another lifetime, old friend. I was a lion who accidentally got stuck in some extremely thick mud and you were the jackal who helped me." (LJJAT)

"Are not jackals low and vulgar creatures, master?"

"Ordinarily they are, Ananda, but in this particular case you and I became excellent friends."

"That is *wonderful,* master."

"Of course, my wife didn't like you and wanted you gone."

"Oh no . . ."

"But do you know what I told her, Ananda? 'This jackal is my friend, wife,' I said, 'no matter how small and weak he is, you should not despise him as you do.' Wasn't that generous of me?"

"Your wife despised me?"

"Oh yes, very much so. But I told her not to."

"Thank you, master. I guess what I was wondering though . . ."

I squeezed his hand, nodded. "Is whether you have ever given your life for me, is that it, old friend?"

"Yes!"

"You have indeed, Ananda."

"Oh, master, I am so glad! Please tell me about it!"

"Once I was a beautiful young man and you, Ananda, were a crab." (BYJAT)

" . . . A crab?"

"Yes, and we became very close friends."

"A beautiful young man and a crab became close friends?"

"Yes. Until an evil crow—and I assume you know who *that* was—"

"Devadatta, master?"

"Precisely, until Devadatta decided that he wanted to feast on my eyeballs."

"Only your eyeballs, master?"

"They were magnificent-looking eyeballs."

"Of course."

"The evil-crow Devadatta then made friends with an evil snake."

"Was that *also* Devadatta, master?"

"No, Ananda, the snake was Mara."

"Ooooohh, *Mara* . . ."

"The two of them, Devadatta and Mara, developed a plan to eat my gorgeous eyeballs. But *you*, Ananda, stopped them by killing them both! Well done, old friend!"

Ananda looked at me, joyful tears streaming down his face. "That is so good to hear, master, oh, I am so very happy at this moment, I wish I was that crab right now so I could save you, so I could . . ." He broke down in tears.

"I know you do, old friend, I know you do."

The next morning, I had Ananda gather my monks around me. With an effort, I spoke to them.

"I wish to announce to all of you that my man Ananda has *four* good qualities. Good quality number one: People are always happy to see Ananda. Good quality number two: People are always unhappy to not see Ananda. Good quality number three . . ." At that point, I stalled, unable to think of any more good qualities that Ananda possessed. My monks stared at me for a long moment, waiting for more, but I finally just closed my eyes and pretended to fall asleep and the moment passed. (MPB 5:16; ANG 4:129–30)

28

The following morning I sat under a tree and meditated. I would die by the end of the day, I knew that. After a moment, a bunch of flowers fell on my head. I was used to flowers falling on my head by now, obviously. I also wasn't surprised when some powders were sprinkled all over me. Honestly, by this time I'd had flowers, powders and ointments dumped on me so many damned times that I hardly even noticed them anymore. What I *did* notice, however, was the song praising me which I heard the gods crooning up in heaven. I glanced over at Ananda and smiled weakly. "Never has the Perfect One been so worshipped and adored, eh, old friend?" He nodded vaguely.

Not long afterwards Ananda was massaging my feet while another monk, Upavana, fanned me. Noticing some gods approaching, I suddenly barked, "Move aside, monk!" at Upavana.

"Why do you speak to Upavana in that harsh way, master?" Ananda asked.

"The gods have arrived to behold me, Ananda, millions of them, possibly even billions. They have traveled a long way and do you know what they are saying to each other at this moment? 'We came to see the Perfect One before he dies but now this idiot monk Upavana is blocking our view!' That's what they are saying!" (MPB 5:3–4)

Ananda nodded slightly to Upavana, who quickly scooted

away. Glancing around, Ananda asked worriedly: "What kind of gods do you *see*, master?" "First of all, I see gods with messy hair, Ananda. They are weeping and crying out, 'Too soon, TOO SOON!!' Secondly, I see gods standing and staring at me and saying, 'Well, everything dies, right?' Which is obviously true, but I do not like those gods very m—UUUHHHHHH." At that point, I was overcome with sudden excruciating pain in my belly and I passed out.

When I woke up, Ananda was sitting next to me, gazing down at me with tears in his eyes.

"You have another question for me, old friend?" I managed.

"This is so difficult, master . . ."

"Go on."

"After you are gone . . . what should we do with your remains, master?"

"It is an excellent question, Ananda, and I am glad you asked it. First of all, I don't want *you* running my funeral, alright?" I lifted my hand, quickly silencing him. "There are others who are more suited for the job, Ananda, that's all I'm going to say. You may, however, give the following instructions to the *sangha*: 'Treat the Perfect One's remains as you would those of a monarch.'"

"What does it mean, master?"

"It means to first wrap my body in linen. Then after that, wrap it in wool, then linen again, then wool again. Then alternate layers of linen and wool a thousand times."

"A *thousand times*, master?"

"Yes. After that, put me into an iron pot. Then put that iron pot into *a second* iron pot. Are you going to remember all this, Ananda?"

"Yes, master, put the first iron pot into a second iron pot."

"After that, build a fire (put lots of perfume in it obviously) and burn me in my pot-within-a-pot. After all that, build a shrine to me. Anyone who leaves flowers at my shrine will be rewarded." (MPB 5:11)

"Will they become gods, master?"

"They will simply 'receive benefits,' Ananda, I'm not going to be any more specific than UUUHHHHHHHH …." Once again, I was suddenly overcome with pain and blacked out.

By that evening, I was moments from death. Before I left this world, however, I had one final disciplinary action to carry out. "Chandaka, my old friend and charioteer?" I whispered to my monks.

"Yes, Tathagata?"

I thought back to the day Chandaka had accompanied me in witnessing the Four Sights—the night he had helped me escape Father's palace—the day he had joined my *sangha*. "*Punish him,*" I croaked, fading fast.

"Punish him, Tathagata?"

"Give him the worst possible penalty."

"But *why*, Tathagata?"

"Because he has favored women. *Ostracize him.*" (MPB 6:4)

"Yes, Tathagata."

I looked around at my monks; their faces were pained, many of them were struggling to maintain composure. I was a minute or two from death, I knew that. "Any final questions for the Tathagata, *bikkhus*?" I whispered. "Anything at all?" A few of them sniffled, but none spoke. "How wonderful that your monks have no questions for you, master," Ananda piped up. "It means they feel no doubt!"

I didn't want to be annoyed with Ananda in the last ninety seconds of my life, I truly didn't, but what he'd said was impertinent. "Understand, Ananda," I rasped out, "that *you* speak merely from faith while *I* know for certain that my monks have no doubt." Ananda nodded sheepishly. (MPB 6:6)

I could feel the final darkness closing in on me. Before I died, I spoke to my monks one final time. "Everything dies," I whispered. "But work hard." "*Perfect,*" I remember thinking as I died. (ANG 4:76)

My death occurred in several stages; I moved from one *jhana* to another until I entered the sphere of Infinite Space, Infinite

Consciousness and Infinite Nothingness and then after that the End, which is the Cessation of All Things.

"My master is *dead*," Ananda moaned miserably at that moment.

"No, Ananda," Anuruddha quickly replied, "he's not 'dead,' he's merely attained Cessation."

At that moment I turned *back* from the End and reentered the realms of Infinite Nothingness, Infinite Consciousness and Infinite Space. I then proceeded to travel back and forth between the Realm of Cessation and the Realm of Infinity several times. To be honest, I'm still not totally sure why I did it. Finally, however, I did die. (MPB 6:8–9; SY 6:15)

29

Not long after my demise, my monks started singing and dancing around my corpse, throwing flowers and dumping perfume all over me. I had never been in favor of singing and dancing in general, obviously, but having these things done around my dead body, well, it was highly undignified, that's all I can say. The monks sang and danced for such a long time that by the time they were worn out it was too late to cremate me. "We'll do it tomorrow," they agreed. But the next day, they instantly started singing and dancing again—and still no cremation. The day after that was the same, as was the next and the next and the next. My monks just kept singing and dancing around me day after day! I was starting to look hideous by this time, a real decomposing mess. Finally someone yelled out, "We've sung and danced enough, let's cremate him!" But before they could do it they all started singing and dancing yet *again*. This time they were joined by the gods, who started doing bizarre "god dances" around my corpse. (A lot of hip gyrations and sinuous arm movements.) (MPB 6:14–16)

Finally, after a week of this nonsense, someone asked Ananda, "What should we do with the Tathagata's body anyway?" "We must wrap the Tathagata in linen," Ananda informed them, "then cover the linen with wool, then alternate linen and wool a thousand times—"

"A *thousand times?*" someone asked.

"Yes, then after that we must put him into an iron pot, burn him up and build a shrine to him." "Not bad, Ananda," I remember thinking to myself, "but you forgot to tell them to put the first iron pot into a second iron pot, which was the most important part!"

After the monks finally cremated me, what was left was nothing but perfect white bones; my flesh had melted away like butter. Even then, however, somewhat unbelievably, my monks started dancing around my *skeleton*—they did it for a week! They posed my skeleton with spears and sang to it. (MPB 6:23) Then they started arguing over my bones. "*We* want the Perfect One's skeleton," one group demanded. "No, *we* want it," another countered. "The Perfect One's skeleton is ours," a third protested. Finally, they decided to break my skeleton into eight pieces (Head/Torso/Right Arm/Left Arm/Right Leg/Left Leg/Right Foot/Left Foot) and divide it up that way. (Somehow during the process of my body being sawed into pieces, one of my teeth got knocked out and ended up in heaven—which I had no problem with. Another part, however, ended up with a bunch of snake-kings, which I did have a problem with.)

After the dismembering of my skeleton was done and the pieces were distributed, a final group showed up demanding a piece of me, but since there was literally nothing left they had to settle for some embers from the fire I'd been burned up in, which I thought was pretty sad for them, honestly. (MPB 6:24) At that point I was ready to move on to my final reward: *Nirvana*. Before I went, however, there was one *last* thing I needed to witness: Ananda's public humiliation. (CV 11:1–10; SY 16:11; THR)

The charges against Ananda were as follows: (1) He had not asked me *nearly* enough questions (true); (2) He had once accidentally stepped on my robe (also true); (3) He had allowed women to observe my naked dead body (true; the way they had cried all over my corpse was frankly repulsive); (4) He had spoken out in favor of women joining the *sangha*, thus cutting its lifespan in half (true); (5) And worst of all by far, he had neglected to beg me to live *forever* (damnably true).

"How do you plead to your charges?" a jury of monks demanded of Ananda.

"I see no fault in what I did, sirs," Ananda responded shakily. "I loved my master, I devoted my whole *life* to him, I do not understand why I am being *punished* in this way. I asked my master endless questions and also I did ask him to live on, *twice* in fact, I simply didn't know I needed to do it a *third* time. If I'd known that, I certainly would've done it! And yes, I did accidentally step on his robe one time, but I didn't mean to do it, it was an accident! As for the women, I will not lie—I genuinely believed they would add to our community."

"Do you confess your guilt or do you not, boy?"

"I have white hair, sir, I am not a boy."

"You ARE a boy," the monk in charge announced, and I nodded firmly to myself, "Put that boy in his damned place."

"You did *not* ask the Perfect One enough questions, boy, do you or do you not acknowledge your guilt?"

Ananda lowered his eyes. "I do accept my guilt, sirs."

"You *did* step on the Perfect One's cloak, boy, do you or do you not acknowledge your guilt?"

Trembling slightly, Ananda nodded. "I do accept my guilt, sirs."

"You took the side of *women*, boy."

Ananda shook his head. "I took the side of the Perfect One's stepmother, sirs. She was his nurse, she fed him from her body when his own mother died. I did not see it as wrongdoing on my part to suggest that she might be included in the *sangha*." The jury of monks stared at Ananda in stunned, horrified silence. Finally, in a wavering voice, Ananda spoke. "Nevertheless, I do accept my guilt, sirs."

"And most of all, boy, *most of all*, when the Perfect One gave you repeated hints that he required you to beg him to live forever, *you did not do it, which makes you—YOU—responsible for his death.* Do you or do you not acknowledge your guilt?"

Ananda began to weep at this point; his whole body shuddered violently. "I was under the influence of Mara, masters, I did not see that at the time but I do now. Mara tricked me, sirs, he tricked me into wickedness, but I do accept my guilt, ohhhh lord I doooooooo . . ."

As Ananda crumpled to the floor and sobbed pitifully, I nodded firmly to myself. "Good," I thought. "That is good."

"And now," I thought, "at long last I achieve my blessed reward—*Extinction.*"

And oh, *bikkhus,* my extinction felt well-deserved indeed.

about the author

Chris Matheson is a screenwriter and author. His film credits include the three *Bill & Ted* movies and *Rapture-Palooza*. His books include *The Story of God* and *The Trouble with God*. He lives in Portland, Oregon.